The Chain Of Life

By

Ronna M. Bacon

You make known to me the path of life; You will fill me with joy in Your presence, with eternal pleasures at Your right hand. Psalm 16:11 NKJV

Table of Contents

Chapter 1
Chapter 2
Chapter 3
Chapter 4
Chapter 5
Chapter 6
Chapter 7
Chapter 8
Chapter 9
Chapter 10
Chapter 11
Chapter 12
Chapter 13
Chapter 14
Chapter 15
Chapter 16
Chapter 17
Chapter 18
Chapter 19
Chapter 20
Chapter 21
Chapter 22
Chapter 23
Chapter 24
Chapter 25
Chapter 26
Chapter 27
Chapter 28
Chapter 29
Chapter 30
Chapter 31

Chapter 32
Chapter 33
Chapter 34
Chapter 35
Chapter 36
Chapter 37
Chapter 38
Chapter 39
Chapter 40
Chapter 41
Chapter 42
Chapter 43
Chapter 44
Chapter 45
Chapter 46
Chapter 47
Chapter 48
Chapter 49
Chapter 50
Chapter 51
Chapter 52
Epilogue
Dear Readers

Chapter 1

The shackles dragging at his ankles, weighing down his steps, the young man paced what he could of the small, damp, dark cell he was captive in. Fatigue and malnutrition added to the factor of how he was managing to barely stay upright. Just in his late twenties, he felt three times that age, he decided. He lifted his hand to rub at his face, feeling the days-old growth of beard that covered his face, the shackles on his wrists clanking as he moved. He had given up, he decided. Life meant nothing to him now. He would die here, he thought, and likely soon.

He stared at the wall, where dark marks had begun to show the length of time he had been held, that was until he gave up and just stopped marking them. What was the use, he decided? No one would ever know. He had no idea or thought as to why he was captive, other than he was a white man in a Central American country who had tangled with looters and been taken captive and placed here, despite his protests to the contrary. He had had no lawyer. Had seen no one other than the man who brought a bowl of watery gruel or soup and a mug of water twice a day.

He had lost weight and with the weight loss, had lost his muscle and stamina. He could barely stand some days. *I wish I had never come here, he thought, but I had to. I had to find her, only I never did. I didn't get a chance to look. The looters overwhelmed me that very first night. And I no longer know how much time had passed.* He threw himself to a sitting position on his pallet, his head drooping as he did so, his arms wrapping around himself to try and warm his body.

He looked up through blurry eyes, a frown on his face as he saw the slight figure who entered, a tray in their hands. This was not his normal guard. He simply dropped his head back down on his chest and slumped even harder against the wall, the paper-thin pallet under him not protecting from the dampness and cold. He could feel the fever building in him and just sighed.

The figure dropped the tray to the floor and then stepped back to the door, a hand out to hold the door open. A second figure entered, reaching for the young man and slinging him over his shoulder, merely pointing back the way they had come. They slipped away, the cell door locked behind them, eyes watching from the other cells, but not one word, not one sound escaped the occupants.

The two figures seemed to merge into one as they left the prison, heading for the jungle that encroached close to the exit they had chosen. The night had cooperated with them, clouds covering the moon and stars. The night creatures helped to cover the sound of their movement, as quiet as it was.

The duo paused at a small creek, the man dropping the prisoner to the ground, as he searched for the hand-carved wooden canoe they had found. He returned with it, reaching for the prisoner and dropping him gently into it, waiting for his companion to jump in, a hand on the man's chest, and then he dropped in as well, reaching for a paddle and with strong swift strokes, taking them away from the prison and towards safety. He paddled throughout the night, soft comments once in a while with his companion before he finally paddled to the shore, and stepped from the canoe, pulling it and out of the water. He reached to help his companion out and then for the prisoner, once more slinging him over his shoulder and then heading back into the jungle. The two kept a watchful eye for dangerous critters, venomous snakes, and insects. They finally stopped in a clearing, near a plane that had been camouflaged with netting.

"Are we safe?" The smaller one, a lady, looked behind her even as she dropped to her knees beside the prisoner, assessing him, shock running through her at how he looked.

"I think so. Let me get the netting off and then we'll take off. It's close enough to dawn I should have enough light." He paused, his eyes on the man. "He's in rough shape. He may not make it."

"God did not take us in there, to let him die before we get him home." She looked up at him, her clear blue eyes like a summer sky, shining in the waning moonlight. "We'll get him out and to Dad. Dad will look after him."

"I'm sure he will, sis." The man stepped away, his hands busy removing and folding the netting to store in the back of the plane, his thoughts on the trip ahead. It was an hours' long one, he thought, and I just don't know if we'll make it in time. He turned back to his sister, his eyes the same hue as hers watching closely. Lord, we made it from the prison. I just don't know if we'll make it home. Please, Lord, don't let this one die on us. The last one took too much from her.

Saoirse Gallagher looked towards her brother, Connell, thinking how glad she was that he was with her. She had travelled with others in their group, but never felt the confidence in them that she had in him.

Once in the plane, their prisoner fastened into a seat, the seatbelt holding him as upright as possible, Connell made quick work of his shackles, tossing them aside before grimacing at the wounds.

"It will take time for those to heal, Saoirse. He'll always have scars."

She nodded, her hands reaching for the saline she needed to help cleanse the wounds and then the bandages to wrap around his wrists and ankles.

"Who does this, Connell? Why?"

"We'll ask him when we can. I didn't know it was him, did you?"

Saoirse shook her head. "No, Dad didn't say. Just said we needed to go in and get out as quickly as we could. It was almost too easy." Her hand rested against the man's forehead. "He has a fever, Connell."

"That I don't doubt." Connell moved away, settling himself into the pilot's seat and going through his pre-flight check. "Buckle up, sis. Let's get away from here and get Rowan Sullivan home to Dad."

The flight uneventful, hours later, Connell gracefully landed his plane, taxiing to the waiting hanger and then pulling to a stop. He turned, his post-flight check done, and rose, stretching for a moment. He always felt cramped when on a long flight, there seemed not enough room for his height.

The door open, he spoke with his father, who stood at the bottom of the stairs that were lowered, just waiting for his daughter to appear.

Saoirse rose, her face troubled. "He's really sick, Connell. I don't know if he'll recover."

Connell hugged his sister before reaching for Rowan, carrying him gently down the stairs to the waiting truck, sliding him onto the back seat, watching with a tinge of amusement as Saoirse slid in the other side, her arms ready to support the man.

Kelly Gallagher stepped forward, ducking his head for a quick assessment, noting the bandages on the wrists and ankles.

"Any trouble, son?"

"No. That puzzles me. We walked in, walked out. None of the prisoners even said anything as we passed by."

"That's strange. God was with you. Our team spent the last twenty-four hours in prayer for you. Now, let's get him to our home and see what we need to do for him."

Connell's hand stopped his father from opening the front passenger's door.

"Dad, why us?"

"What do you mean, why us?"

"There are others who could have gone in and rescued him. Why us?"

Kelly drew a deep breath. "I know his father, Ronan. We were childhood friends and lost touch in our thirties. He contacted me a week ago, having determined just where his son was. He told me we were the only ones he would ask, that if we refused, he would go in on his own. I couldn't let him do that."

"No, I guess you couldn't. It just seems strange. Do we know why he was there?"

Kelly hesitated again. "We do. Saoirse had been there a few months ago with the mission. Somehow, Rowan heard about that and for some reason thought she was in danger. He flew down to try and find her, his father said. Rowan told him he had to do it for us."

"He did? But Saoirse wasn't in any danger, not that we know of."

"But she was, Connell. She was. I found that out after she came home. That was one reason I hesitated to let her go back." Kelly stared up at his son, just a few inches taller than him, sharing the same deep auburn hair as his sister and with the same clear blue eyes. "Let's get home, son. That man there needs our help even now."

Chapter 2

Saoirse watched as Connell carried Rowan up the outside stairs to the large house that they inhabited, her hand holding the back door open for him before she let it swing closed behind them. She could hear her mother in the spare room that Connell was heading for.

Kelly stopped her with a hand on her arm, watching her closely. He could see the strain on her face and sighed. *Lord? Why Saoirse? What did she see or not see down there? Did she bring something back that she should not have? I am at a loss to know.*

"Go, get cleaned up, love." He shook his head at her look of protest. "No, your work is finished for now. Mom will look after him with Connell's help." His wife, Ruth, was a family physician. Connell was a firefighter. "Go on. I'll have breakfast waiting for you when you come back."

Saoirse finally nodded, fatigue weighing down her eyes. Her steps dragged as she headed for the hallway to the room that she was using at present. She had moved home not that long again, giving up her freedom. She had been terrified recently, sure that someone had been in her apartment and moving things around. She just didn't have any evidence of that. Elmton used to feel so safe. At the moment? It didn't to her. She had prayed for safety, for peace, and still felt a great unease.

Turning as Connell helped Rowan back from a shower and then into clean clothes, Ruth watched Rowan carefully and then her own son. This was almost beyond her skills, she thought, compassion on her face as she watched the younger man sigh and settle down into the bed, Connell pulling the covers up over him and tucking them around him before he stepped back.

"Mom?" Connell didn't have the words to express his anger, his fear, or his concern.

"Did he say anything at all, Connell?" She reached for her stethoscope and moving to sit on the side of the bed before looking up at her son.

Connell shook his head. "Not a word, Mom. Not a word. His eyes are vacant."

"He's been through trauma, Connell. That happens. He's shut down to protect himself, I suspect." Ruth quickly did an assessment before she was on her feet, reaching for an IV needle, line and bag of fluid. "I'll get this started and see how that works." She frowned as she turned back to Rowan. "What conditions did you find him in?"

Giving a rough laugh, Connell stared down at Rowan.

"It was primitive, Mom. A prison out in the jungle. Far away from civilization or what is known as that. Shackles on his wrists and ankles. A few blankets on the floor. We found the trays waiting for them to go to the prisoners. Some thin soup or whatever. A mug of dirty water. That is all. The cell itself? Damp. Dark. Alive with vermin."

Ruth nodded, her concentration on Rowan as she assessed his vital signs. She was on her feet, reaching for the syringes and vials that she needed to draw blood.

"I know you're exhausted, but you're known at the lab. Can you run this in for me?" Ruth reached for the requisition that was needed. "Did he have any identification on him?"

Connell moved to the attached bathroom and back with Rowan's wallet. "He did, Mom. Here, I'll let you look through it for what you need." A frown crossed his face. "That's odd, Mom. He still had his wallet, his cell phone, and his passport. That doesn't make sense."

"No, it doesn't make sense." Ruth frowned as she completed the requisition and labelled the vials. "Here you go, son. Off with you if you will. Then, Dad will have your breakfast. You'll need to sleep."

"I will, Mom. It's not that far to the lab." Connell hesitated, his mouth open to ask a question before he snapped it closed and was off. His thoughts were dark. What did Dad mean, he wondered, that Saoirse was in danger? I don't see that.

Kelly watched as Connell slipped silently from the house before he stood in the hallway staring towards Saoirse's room. He shook his head. No sign of her yet. He walked towards the bedroom where he could hear Ruth moving quietly around and watched from the doorway for a moment before he moved towards her. Ruth turned into his arms, welcoming his hug.

"How is he?" Kelly watched as Rowan just lay without moving, a hand on his chest, the other tucked under the blankets.

"It's so strange, Kelly." Ruth turned in his arms to study Rowan. "He's quiet. Not speaking. I didn't find any injuries other than where the shackles were and they're not as bad as I thought. But he just doesn't respond. Connell mentioned that his eyes seemed vacant."

"They would be. We both know why."

"We do. I hate this when it happens, Kelly. All we can do is treat him physically and then pray for him."

"Prayer will work miracles. That I don't doubt." Kelly's head tilted for a moment. "He looks like Ronan."

"He does. Connell said that he'll trim the beard and shave it later. We'll need Saoirse to trim his hair."

"We do, but not right now." Kelly turned as he heard a noise in the kitchen. "Come out when you can, sweetheart. I have a meal ready for us."

Kelly turned to walk away, stopping to look at Ruth as she laid a hand on his arm.

"Ruth?"

"Saoirse? How has this affected her?" Ruth was concerned about their daughter.

"I don't know. I'll speak with her but she's become so quiet lately, it's hard to know if she'll even open up."

Ruth nodded. "Something happened that made her move home, Kelly. And she has not said what."

"No. I asked Connell if she had and he said no." Kelly hesitated, thinking through the timeline. "That was just after she was down there, wasn't it?"

"It was. Kelly, we need to cover her with prayer." Ruth was suddenly deeply afraid for their daughter.

Chapter 3

Setting down on the table the glass of orange juice that she had poured for herself, Saoirse dished up a plate of scrambled eggs, eyeing them before she reached for the ketchup. Today, she needed ketchup on them. Ground pepper was added to the mix. She reached for the rye toast that she preferred, slathering the two pieces with butter before she turned to the table and set the plate down. Her head bowed over her meal, Saoirse prayed for her food and then for the young man in their home.

Kelly rested his hand on her head for a moment and prayed for his daughter even as he moved past her to fix his own plate of food. He sat, his head bowed for a moment before he began to eat. Saoirse watched her father, waiting for him to speak.

"Dad?"

Saoirse's voice brought Kelly back to the present and he looked up at his daughter.

"Dad? How is he?" Saoirse was worried.

"He's resting, love. Mom has started an IV for him and sent off blood work. It will be a while, she thinks, before he rouses."

Saoirse let out a deep breath, deep enough that her body moved with it.

"I'm worried, Dad. You didn't see the conditions that we found him in. Did he say anything?"

"No, not that I know of." Kelly pointed at her plate of food with his fork. "Eat up. Mom will be out shortly."

Tucking the blankets tighter around Rowan, Ruth worried. *Not just about his physical wellbeing,* she thought. *His mental health will be at stake. I agree with Connell. He has shut down. And I have no way of knowing how to bring him back. Lord, You*

———

16

are the Great Physician. You will need to step in, to heal this young man.

Ruth stood for a moment in the hallway, her eyes on her daughter before she moved into the room, sitting as Kelly motioned her to do so. He rose to dish up her plate of food, setting it before her, his gaze flickering between his wife and daughter. Saoirse just sat, eating, her gaze on her plate. That she was deeply troubled, Kelly knew. Just why though was the question that they had not been able to get an answer for.

Connell moved through the kitchen as well, his own plate of food on the table before he reached to refill his parents' coffees and Saoirse's juice. He shook his head at his mother, his eyes going back to Saoirse. They would need to talk, he knew, but now was not the time.

"How is he, Mom?" Connell's voice finally broke through the silence.

"About the same. We'll need to start getting him sitting up and drinking broth and water and juice as we can." Ruth sighed, knowing that they had a gigantic task ahead of them. "You're back to work tomorrow, aren't you?"

Connell nodded. "I am. Early shift so I can help in the afternoon. I ran into Silas earlier. He's on his way over with Madigan."

"Oh, good. We can use their help." Kelly cleared the table before he sat back down, his hands reaching out for his wife and daughter's even as Connell did the same. They always spent time in prayer when gathered as a family. It was a custom that Kelly and Ruth had started as newlyweds and just kept up over the years.

Saoirse finally rose, heading for the guest bedroom, to stand in the doorway. Her eyes were on Rowan as he slept, moving his head slightly as he did so. She sighed once more. *Lord, I don't get it. I just don't get why he was there. I know what Dad has said but how did he hear about me?*

Finally moving towards her favourite room in the house, Saoirse reached into a wooden chest under a wide window in the sunroom. She pulled a jade and cream velour blanket that she used to cover herself as she curled up on a wicker love seat. She was asleep before she had really gotten settled down. Ruth watched for a moment before she reached to straighten the blanket over her daughter, fear suddenly hitting her in a huge wave.

Chapter 4

Watching her friend closely as she slept, Madigan Peters finally moved to sit in one of the wicker rockers, her hand resting on her swelling abdomen. She and her husband, Silas, pastor to the church, were expecting their little one in a few months and some days she tired quickly. Today was one of those days but she would never admit it. Mads, as she was known to her friend, studied Saoirse, seeing the stress and strain on her friend's face, in the lines that were becoming deeply drawn. She didn't like the grayness that underlined that or the whiteness either.

Saoirse finally stirred, sitting up and pushing at the hair that had come loose from her braid. She had often thought of cutting her hair but loved the length of it, the hair reaching to her waist when loose. She was surprised to see Madigan sitting there, her head back and her eyes closed.

Standing, Saoirse moved from the room heading towards the bedroom to check on Rowan. She watched from the doorway as her father helped Rowan sip from a mug and then set the mug to one side. She caught the faint nod that Rowan gave before he slipped away to sleep again

Kelly turned as he heard a faint movement, his arm coming out to beckon his daughter close. Wrapping her into his hug, he waited, knowing that she would speak when she was ready.

"Dad? How is he?"

"Mom checked on him a while ago. She said it was good that she was home today, it being Saturday. We've been able to get some fluids down him."

Saoirse's head was against her father. "Do we know why he was there?"

Kelly sighed, his eyes on Connell as he had approached to stand on the other side of the bed.

"We do, love. We do. It was you."

"Me?" Saoirse's voice rose in surprise before she clamped her mouth closed. "I don't understand."

"His father, Ronan, and I go back to being friends as youngsters. We lost contact over the years until he approached me last week. He asked that we go in and find Rowan and bring him home. Other than that, he would go in on his own. I couldn't let him do that." Kelly grew silent, his mind on the conversation with his old friend. "Rowan went there because of you, Saoirse."

"Me? I don't understand, Dad. I don't know him. Have never met him."

"No, you haven't. Rowan told his father that you were in danger and that he had to go and find you and protect you. For me. He flew down there before his father could stop him. In fact, he called his father from the airport just as he was catching his flight."

"I still don't understand, Dad. What danger?"

Connell shared a look with his father before he gave a slight shake of his head.

"Ronan didn't know, Saoirse. He just said Rowan left to find you." Connell looked at his father again. "Ronan and Lydia are here, Dad."

"Thanks, son. Come on, you two. You need to meet Ronan and Lydia." Kelly hesitated at the look on Saoirse's face, not sure what she was thinking.

"I'll be out shortly, Dad. Mads is here and I need to find her." Saoirse was gone before her father could stop her.

"She'll blame herself, Dad." Connell moved to the doorway to watch her.

"I know. We can't help that, son. All we can do is pray. And investigate what he was thinking. And that we don't know."

"I ran into Bill and Cora when I was out. He asked what we were up to. He's going to stop by later tonight, just as a friend, to see what he can do to help."

"Good. Now, let's find Rowan's parents and then get them in to see him." Kelly paused in the doorway, turning to study the young man sleeping. He shook his head. *Lord, I have no idea what he was thinking or even doing, other than he was that concerned about my girl. Heal him in all ways, Lord.*

Chapter 5

Ronan Sullivan turned from where he was staring out the front window of the living room, his hand outstretched to shake that of his long-time friend.

"Kelly! It's good to see you. I just wish the circumstances were different."

"And you as well, Ronan. I am sorry that we lost touch, other than for the Christmas cards we have exchanged. It shouldn't have happened."

"No, it shouldn't have. That's life, Kelly. We move on and away from people. Lydia, you remember Kelly?" Ronan reached out a hand for his wife.

"I do." Lydia moved to her husband's side before she reached to hug Kelly. "Thank you, Kelly."

Kelly shrugged. "It was my kids that went in."

"But it was you who arranged it. Trained them too."

Kelly merely shrugged again, a small smile on his face. "You only have Rowan?"

"We do. God decided that we should have only one, but we did foster for a while." Ronan's voice stopped before his eyes slid closed. "One of the foster boys was from that country. Is there a connection?"

"I wasn't aware of that. It's possible." Kelly pointed towards the kitchen. "It's almost suppertime and I know Ruth has a meal ready. Connell is there, I do believe." He introduced the couple to his son and then turned. "Saoirse?"

"Still in the sunroom with Madigan, Dad. Silas snuck in through the door there." Connell grinned. "He hasn't changed."

"No, he hasn't." Kelly laughed. "Silas and Madigan are our pastoral couple. You will like them, I think." He watched as Connell moved to go and find them.

Ruth looked around. "We could eat in the dining room, Kelly."

"The kitchen is fine, Ruth." Lydia was quick to reassure her. "That's where we eat at home unless it's a special occasion."

"All right, then. Kelly, we'll need the board in to extend the table." Ruth moved around, dishing up their meal, listening to the talk, before she moved away, heading to find Rowan still asleep, a flushed look to his face. *Please, Lord, no fever! I would have to admit him and that means the care would go to someone else. I am not sure that would be good given that we don't know who it is yet.*

Saoirse stood beside her for a moment, Silas on the other side of the bed, his eyes on the younger man. *Lord, I sense that Saoirse is still in grave danger. We need this man to awake and be able to explain to us why he went to that country and just what danger that he thought our friend is in. I sense as well, dear Lord, that it will be a while. Heal his body and mind.*

Silas nodded as Ruth looked over at him. "We'll pray, Ruth. We'll pray. I'll put out an unspoken request to the church for you and this situation. Our church doesn't need to know the details. They will pray for you all."

"Thank you, Silas. We have been blessed with such an understanding and caring pastor. Now, let's go eat. Saoirse, that means you too. You need to eat." Ruth would not let her daughter stay, as much as she wanted to. "His parents are here and you will meet them."

Saoirse studied the Sullivans as they ate, listening as they caught up on their life stories with her parents. She didn't realize that Ronan kept shooting glances at her but both Connell and Silas caught them. The two younger men exchanged glances as well before Connell shook his head. He had no idea what Saoirse had become involved in but he feared for her. His heart cried out in prayer for her.

———

23

Ronan and Lydia followed Ruth to the bedroom, stopping at the foot of the bed, Lydia's hand covering her mouth before she was on her knees beside her son. Her hand reached to touch his face, causing him to twist somewhat before his eyes flickered but didn't stay open. Ronan was on his knees on the other side, tears on his face. His hand was on his son's, his grasp tight. To say that he was shocked at Rowan's look would have been an understatement. He could hear Lydia's soft sobs and prayed for them all. *Lord, please? We need to know what happened. And I am not at all sure that Rowan can or will tell us. He didn't say much, Lord, in that call other than to tell me where he was going, asking for my prayers and blessings. And how could I say no?*

Chapter 6

Day by day, Rowan began to rouse, to acknowledge with a nod or slight smile the care that he was being given. Connell had finally shaved him at his request. Saoirse had trimmed his hair, a sheet draped over him as Connell helped him stay upright. Ronan had watched that day, seeing the tenderness with which Saoirse had worked around Rowan, her touch gentle. He frowned somewhat at the look on her face before he shrugged. *Lord, I can't read her thoughts but You can. Guide them, Lord, as they look for answers.*

Bill Buckley, a detective on the town force, had been around as he had promised, taking down notes and promising to look into the situation. He couldn't promise, though, that he would find out much. He had talked privately with Saoirse about what she had been going through.

Saoirse had shrugged, handing him her keys to the apartment. She still had a few weeks left on her lease and was gradually clearing out the apartment. There was still a good amount of furniture there. Bill had looked at her and then hugged her, the ease of old friends in his touch. He had promised that he would clear it out for her, with Andrew McBeth's help. Andrew was the chief of police but also a good friend to the family. Silas had already approached her about that.

"Thank you, Bill. I don't want any of it. I just can't." She had looked at him, a distressed look on her face.

Bill had nodded. "I understand. Now, Cora wants you to come for a meal. When will you?"

She had looked at him and then shrugged. "Sometime this week?"

"Tomorrow. I am looking forward to that as I know Cora is. Our little fellow heard us talking about you and is so excited

———

25

that his friend will be coming to visit him." Bill had grinned as he remembered his son's excitement.

"I missed him when I was away. And I haven't been in the nursery a lot at church lately. Other duties that I am giving up. I miss the little ones."

The next afternoon, Bill stood outside the apartment door, a stern look on his face as he stared at it. He sighed. They wouldn't be packing up the furniture and whatnot and clearing out the apartment, not for a while. He pulled out his phone before he turned at a touch on his shoulder. One of the crime lab techs stood beside him.

"Saoirse's?" The tech shook his head.

"That's right, Walter. I was just about to call it in. We need the team to go through here." Bill pointed to the door. "Someone has been around and I don't think Saoirse would have done this." There were fresh scratches around the lock, gouging into the wood, and when Bill touched the door, it swung slightly open.

Two hours later, Connell approached Bill as he stood by his truck.

"Bill? Any word on when we can go in?" Connell was worried about his sister and this didn't help. He looked back towards his own truck, seeing Saoirse standing outside of it, her arms wrapped around herself.

"It's clear for us to go in." Bill's voice was grim. He sighed. "Your sister's here?"

"She is. I brought her even though she didn't want to be here. You need her to go through the place?"

"I do." Bill turned, finding Saoirse standing beside her brother. "Saoirse, we need to talk. You were not imagining anything. Walter took his team through." Bill pointed towards the apartment. "Let's go in and I'll explain what we found."

"Do I want to?" Saoirse's face was white.

"You need to. This is not a game, Saoirse, and your life is in danger."

———

Her face whitened ever further. "You found something?" Distress showed in her eyes and both men picked up on the fear that she felt.

"A lot of somethings." Bill exchanged a grim look with Connell, seeing the worry in his friend's eyes for his sister. "Come on. It's safe. Walter and his team have pulled everything that they needed to."

Connell wrapped an arm around his sister, his prayer whispering in her ear, even as he walked her towards the apartment. She hesitated at the door before she entered, a hand covering her mouth as she stared at the living room wall.

Chapter 7

Staring at the wall, Saorise's hand covered her mouth, her other hand still tight in her brother's. Connell's face grew even sterner as he studied the words.

Where is it? The words were spray-painted on the wall in fluorescent green, large and commanding to the room.

"I don't know what they want." Saoirse's voice held tears. "I don't. I don't have anything other than my own things." She turned abruptly, tearing her hand from her brother and almost ran through the apartment, seeing the same question in every room.

Connell bent and picked up the leg from a smashed chair in the kitchen before he stared around at the furniture.

"This is brutal, Bill."

"It is." Bill stood where he could watch Saoirse as she wandered the rooms. "She has no idea?"

"If she says she doesn't, she doesn't. We've been friends for years. You know that she would admit to it if she had something."

"I know." Bill turned as he heard a sound at the door. "Andrew?"

"Bill? What is going on?" Andrew stood, staring around the rooms before he walked to stand in front of the wall. "This looks familiar, Bill."

"That's what I thought." Bill turned for a moment, watching as Connell hugged his sister. "We'll need to talk to her. She was to come for a meal tonight with Cora and me. Now, I'm not so sure that's a good idea."

"She needs this. I talked to Kelly. He indicated that Rowan headed down south to find Saoirse. He told his father that she was in trouble. We need to talk to him, to find out what he was thinking and what information he has.”

“And that could be a problem.” Bill shook his head. “He’s not talking. Connell said he’s shut down and no one can get him to rouse much. Other than Saoirse. Ruth told Connell that when Saoirse is around him, his eyes follow her and he frowns as if he’s trying to remember something.”

“That’s what I thought Ruth had told me. She’s concerned and I can’t say as I blame her too much. The unknown weighs on them. We both know how that is.” Both Bill and Andrew had been in danger as had their wives, both just escaping death trying to protect them.

Bill nodded. “I’ll head that way once we’re through in here. There isn’t anything to salvage.”

“There’s not?” Andrew walked through the apartment, shaking his head before he stood in front of Saoirse. “Saoirse?”

“Who does this, Andrew? I haven’t done anything to anyone.” He could see the tears that she was fighting to hold back. “I don’t have anything that anyone would want. Not a thing.”

Connell kept his arm around her. “We’ll think this through, sis. We’ll think it through. You’ll need to go through what you brought back from down south.”

“I have, Connell. I have nothing other than what I took down there. I made sure of that. Dad has that drilled into us.”

“I know, sis. I know. We’ll just look over everything again. Bill will want to be there, I suspect.”

“He needs to be, Saoirse.” Andrew’s words, though kindly, were stern. “It’s now an investigation.” He turned to look around. “Madigan’s family will be through to clean up and repaint.” Madigan’s parents had a disaster response company and would take care of the apartment for her. “Bill said that they have canvassed the neighbours. No one heard anything.”

“That doesn’t surprise me. They keep to themselves. If it was during the day, no one is home. They all work.” Saoirse moved to the living room, staring at the wall. “I just don’t get it.”

———

29

"We'll need you to think back to when you were there before you left and after you returned." Bill stared at Saoirse until she nodded in understanding. "I'm sorry, Saoirse. We didn't expect this."

"No, you didn't. But I did and I don't know why." Saoirse turned and ran from the apartment, gone from their sight before any of the men could stop her.

Connell ran after her, not finding her.

"Saoirse, where are you?" His words were low, knowing that he would not find her. She could hide and hide well when she wanted to. This was one time that he suspected she would hide from them all.

Chapter 8

Saoirse stood in the doorway to the sunroom, coming in from the outside before she closed the door and then stood inside, her back against it. She watched Rowan as he sat slumped in one of the wicker rockers that was pulled up near the gas fireplace. She knew her mother would have lit it against the chill in the room. His eyes were closed but she wasn't sure if he was asleep or not.

Dropping down into a matching chair, Saoirse's toe pushed at the floor, sending her chair to rocking. She sighed, slowing the speed at which she was rocking. She was upset and that meant movement for her. She had always been like that.

Ruth stood for a moment, watching her daughter before she shook her head. *Lord, be with our girl. I have no idea why I have such a heavy burden and almost terror for her. Protect her. Let us solve whatever it is that she has become involved in and quickly.* She moved quietly into the room, setting down the glass of juice in her hand on the table beside Rowan. Saoirse watched her mother and sighed herself. I need to talk with her and I'm not sure how.

"Saoirse?" Ruth settled down onto the love seat, her hands idle in her lap.

"Mom? When Bill arrived at my apartment, it had been broken into. He went through it and then had me go in." Saoirse paused, a shudder of fear running through her.

"What happened, dear?"

"It was horrible, Mom. There was a sentence spray-painted on a wall in every room. The furniture was all broken to bits." Saoirse bit at her lip. "Bill had a team go through, he said, and Andrew said Madigan's folks would come in and clean it up. Why?"

—

31

"Why? That's a good question, dear." Ruth's hands rubbed together. "You have no idea? What was the sentence?"

"I don't, Mom. I really don't. The sentence? "Where is it?" I have no idea of what they meant." Her head went back as her eyes closed, not seeing that Rowan's head had raised and that he was watching her, his eyes still dull.

"I see. And I know that you would not have brought anything back with you. That's a standard procedure for us." Ruth's thoughts drifted to when Saoirse had returned. "You were there for what, three days?" At her daughter's nod, she continued. "Connell wasn't with you that time. He was on duty and couldn't go." Ruth finally sighed. "Did we go over the plane?"

"Not that I know of." Saoirse shuddered, fear suddenly hitting her. "Connell might have."

"I didn't, sis." Connell spoke from the entrance to the room. "I'm heading that way now with Bill and Walter. Bill wants to postpone your meal with them."

"I think it's a good idea." Saoirse was on her feet. "I'm coming with you." She stopped as Connell's hand went up. "What? I can't?"

"No, not if it becomes a crime scene. And it might well be. Bill suspects that something may have been hidden on the plane." Connell's eyes were on Rowan, a frown between his eyes as he watched the younger man. "Rowan?"

Rowan's head swung his way before he shook his head. "I'm sorry. I don't know." He rose, shuffling from the room.

The three watched him leave before Connell walked after him.

"Rowan?" Connell waited until Rowan was seated on the bed. "What happened down there?"

Rowan shook his head. "I don't remember. I don't remember going down there or why I did. Dad said that I was worried about your sister. I have never met any of you, not that I know of. So why did I go?"

———

Connell propped a shoulder against the doorframe, knowing that Bill would wait for him. "You don't remember anything?"

"No, I don't. I gave up. That much I know. I didn't think anyone would come for me." Rowan looked up at Connell, a flicker of hope in his eyes. "Why did you come for me?"

"Because your father asked Dad to go in and bring you out. He would have gone himself. Dad refused to let him. Do you know that they were childhood friends? That your Dad is from this town?"

"I knew that he was from this town, I guess. I remember him talking about your parents. I just don't remember meeting them." Rowan crawled back into bed, pulling the covers over him. "I hate this, Connell. I hate not remembering. I hate this way I am feeling."

"We know you do, Rowan. You've muttered that in your sleep." Connell paused. "We'll talk again, Rowan, and I do mean that." Connell walked away, not seeing Rowan staring after him, a frown on his face.

Chapter 9

Seated in the pilot's seat of the cargo plane, Connell looked around. *No,* he thought, *everything here is just as it should be. We don't use this plane a lot except when we have cargo to deliver for the medical missions that need our help. Dad makes sure that it's available when needed.* He rose, heading to stand in the centre of the plane, watching as Walter and his team searched.

Bill entered from where he had just walked up the stairs and came to stand beside him.

"Have they would anything?"

Connell shrugged. "I have no idea if they have. They are keeping quite blank faces if you must know."

Bill grinned. "I am sure that they are. Come on, let's head out. Walter will be down shortly, I suspect. What about the other planes? Were they used at all to go down there?"

Connell shook his head. "No. Just the small jet when we went down there to rescue Rowan." He looked around. "We're being watched, Bill."

"I know that we are. The suspects always do that." Bill grinned again. "I need to warn your sister."

"No need to do that. She's highly aware of that. She's been edgy and nervous." Connell ran his hand through his hair. "I talked with Rowan before we left the house. He doesn't remember much about being there, other than that he gave up."

"I see. Hopefully though over time, he will remember." Bill stared around. "Which is the jet that you used?"

"This one." Connell pointed before he walked towards it, reaching to pull down the stairs and then walking up them. "Dad has been using it for short flights." Kelly ran a courier service that involved not only parcels but passengers. "He hasn't been doing a lot though, given the situation with Saoirse. He's sticking mostly to parcels."

"Is he? Did he have any parcels going out of the country that he was concerned about?"

Connell thought for a moment before he shook his head. "Not that he has said. You would need to speak with him."

"And I will." Bill turned as he heard his name called. "I'll be back." He was gone before Connell could respond.

Standing on the tarmac, the jet's stairs put away, Connell watched as Bill and Walter spoke before Walter ran for the van he was driving and disappeared. Bill seemed to be lost in thought for a few minutes before he walked back towards Connell.

"Bill? I don't like the look." Connell approached him.

"No, I didn't think you would. Walter found four packages on the plane that don't seem to belong to you. He's taken them into the lab." Bill held up a hand. "We had a warrant. Andrew made sure of that."

"I know that. I'm just surprised that he found anything." Connell sighed, the sigh seeming to come from his feet. "There is something then."

"There appears to be. I need to speak with your sister again." Bill pointed to his car. "In and we'll do that."

Connell hunted the house for Saoirse, not finding her. He stood, running a hand through his hair, staring around the yard before he turned back to the house.

"Mom?" Ruth turned from the desk in her office at his voice. "Where's Saoirse? Bill is wanting to talk with her."

"She walked out about thirty minutes ago. And no, I didn't ask where she is going. She's an adult, son, and doesn't have to tell us where she is going." A hand went up at Connell's protest. "We can't, son, not unless we know for sure that she is in imminent danger."

"I know, Mom. It's just that Walter found some things on the cargo plane and Bill wanted to speak with her."

"I'm sorry, son. She's not here. Now, I have reports to finished." Ruth's attention went back to her paperwork, not seeing her son pause and then turn to go and find Bill.

"She's not here, Bill."

"Running is she?" Bill gave a quick grin. "They all do that, only it's usually later in their adventure."

"No, I don't think she is. She's not a runner."

"She will be, Connell." The two men turned as they heard Rowan's voice from behind them. He stood, a hand resting against the wall, his face white with fatigue. "She can only take so much and then she'll run. I don't think that you'll be able to stop her."

"No, I don't think so." Bill studied the younger man. "Have you remembered anything?"

Rowan shook his head. "No, and I wish I could. Dad went through my phone for me, my laptop, my apartment. He could find nothing that raised any concern."

"So why then did you go down there? Your father seemed to think it was spur of the moment." Bill was pressing and they all knew it.

Rowan shrugged, a pained look on his face. "I don't know and I wish I did. Look, I'll unlock my laptop. You can search it if you want."

Bill shook his head. "Not at this time. Maybe at some point." He turned. "Tell Saoirse to call me."

"I will but don't expect it." Connell watched Bill walk away.

———

Chapter 10

Standing in the line at the local coffee shop that she preferred, Saoirse felt uncomfortable. She shifted from foot to foot, an unusual movement for her. She quickly placed her order and then picked it up, turning to move away from the crowds and to the outdoors. Preferring the outdoors had become strong with her in the last few weeks. Saoirse could not understand that.

Turning as she heard a call, a smile lit up her face as Cora approached her.

"Cora? I thought our dinner was off."

Cora snorted. "That's what Bill wanted. But I say it's on. I see you have your coffee. Wait until I grab one and then we'll find somewhere to talk."

"I don't feel that I'm that safe a person to be around right now." Saoirse stared at her friend as she began to laugh.

"You know what Bill and I went through. So I know somewhat how you feel." Cora was away and then back shortly. "How be we head to our place? I do have a meal in the works."

"I would like that, Cora. I need that." Saoirse headed for her vehicle, not seeing the man standing watching her before he too headed for a car.

Bill looked around as he heard Cora entering their home, their little son struggling to get down from his father's arms. William Michael Buckley Junior ran for his mother, throwing himself into her arms and then covering her face with kisses even as she laughed. Michael, as he was known by, hugged her and then spied Saoirse watching him, a grin on her face.

"Sha! Sha's here." He struggled to get down. "Sha, you here." He grinned as she swept him into her arms and hugged him.

"I am. Sha is here. I have come for a meal. Did you cook?"

He frowned at her before he began to giggle and then shake his head. "Mommy did. Daddy too."

"Daddy cooked? Can we eat it?"

Michael frowned at her again and then giggled. "Eat." He was down and away from her, running for the kitchen.

A grin on his face, Bill approached Saoirse. Giving her a hug, he turned her towards the kitchen where he could hear Cora and Michael.

"Casting doubt on my chef abilities?"

Saoirse grinned. "Not at all. It's called putting off the inevitable."

"The inevitable? And that would be?"

"The conversation that I know you want to have with me. Cora, what can I do to help?"

Bill stared after her before he grinned again, shaking his head. *She's got me there, Lord, doesn't she? How do I do this? How do I ask the questions that I need to and not cause her to fear more than she is already? I would ask that You lead in this, Lord.*

Bill listened as Michael chattered away to his mother as she carried him from the kitchen after the meal, a smile on his face. Saoirse watched him, envious she thought. *That's what I want. Someone to love me like I am the only one in the world. A little one to love me just because.*

Bill turned back to his guest, catching the wistful look on her face.

"Saoirse?"

Saoirse shook her head, bringing herself back to the present.

"It's okay, Bill. Now, you wanted to speak with me and I ran."

"You did. You needed to, that much I know." He was up and out of the room, returning with his laptop and a file folder. "Before we look at this, may I pray with you?"

"You may. I need all those prayers, Bill. Somehow, I know I am facing something that I don't want to."

"You are, Saoirse. I think it will be a while until we figure everything out. And I don't want that for you."

Saoirse finally sat back, her eyes on Bill, just waiting for him to speak. He grinned at her silence.

"Not going to ask? Okay. Connell let us go over the cargo plane that you used when you took those supplies down earlier in the year. We did it in a legal manner, search warrants and all, just to prepare if there is ever a court case."

"And will there be?" Saoirse's voice was low, her eyes on Bill.

"There may be, Saoirse. There may well be." He tapped the folder. "These are photos of what we found in the plane." He slid the folder towards her but kept his hand on it. "Connell has not seen these. As it involves you, we need to speak with you."

"I understand that, Bill." Saoirse drew in a deep breath. "Okay. Let me look."

Chapter 11

Drawing in a deep breath, Saoirse opened the folder, her eyes on the photos. A frown puckered her forehead as she paged through the folder.

"I don't recognize any of these. In fact, I would safely say that I have never seen them before. What are they? Artifacts?"

"That they are. One of our techs remembered seeing a notice about stolen artifacts. He's really into the ancient stuff from that era and area. He is concerned, Saoirse, that you will be blamed for removing them." Bill watched her closely.

"I can see that. I don't know who is responsible but it is not me. I was only on the mission site while I was there, except when we were transported there and then back to the plane. I can't see Simon being involved in this."

"We are looking into everyone who was involved here and on the mission team. But it could have been anyone." Bill turned to a folder on his laptop. "I have names that I need to clarify with you. Who they are. What their job descriptions are. How you know them. That sort of information."

An hour later, Saoirse sat back, drained.

"This is hard work, Bill." She reached for the glass of water that Cora had set near her before she left the kitchen.

"It is. You have a good memory, Saoirse. Always have had. I can work with what you have given me. And then we'll talk some more." His face grew stern. "I can't emphasize enough that you need to be extra careful. They will be looking for those parcels. I am surprised that they hadn't been found."

"Dad has security on site all the time. They wouldn't have been able to get to the plane." Saoirse glanced at the clock. "I need to run if there is nothing more that you need. I have to be in early tomorrow at the hangar."

"Sure. Let me walk you out." Bill did just that, admonishing her to send him a text when she got home. Her *Yes, Dad, I will* have him smiling as he watched her drive away.

Saoirse found her favourite spot in the backyard, a swing hidden from sight. She plopped down on it, fatigue in her very movement. Thinking back over Bill's questions, she shook her head. *I just don't know, Lord. I just don't know. Not any more. I used to be so confident and ready to face life. Now? I just want to hide and that's not me. Please, Lord? Let me get back to where I was.*

Rowan hesitated as he approached, not sure if he would be welcome. He stopped yards from her, waiting until she looked up, startled.

"I'm sorry. I didn't mean to scare you."

"You didn't." Saoirse slid over and patted the seat beside her. "Sit. You look like you are going to fall over if you don't."

Rowan gave a small grin as he did just what she had ordered him to do. "I might. Connell was looking for you earlier."

"He was? That's okay. Bill found me. In fact, I had a meal with Bill, his wife, and his little son." Her face softened as she remembered little Michael.

"You did? I'm glad." Rowan grew silent, the habit of the past months deeply ingrained in him.

"Rowan?" Saoirse waited until he looked at her. "Why?"

"Why? Why what?" Rowan shifted so that he could watch her face in the dimming light. He frowned as he saw the stress showing on it and suddenly wished that he could remove it from her.

"Why what? Why did you go down there?" Saoirse rubbed at her face. "I'm sorry. I know that you don't remember."

"I wish that I did. I can't. I have no idea. And that bothers me more than you might imagine."

Saoirse nodded. "I'm sure it does." She sighed. "Then, I guess I'll just have to start looking into it."

"Don't, Saoirse." She spun to stare at him, startled at the stern tone in his voice.

"And why not?"

"Because you are still in danger. You don't know who is after you."

"No, I don't." She sighed. "I'm sorry. I feel responsible for how you are."

Rowan shook his head. "No. I wanted to go and find you. I was driven to do that. At least, I think I was." His brow furrowed as he tried to remember. "I just can't remember."

"Leave it. It's not that long since we brought you home." Saoirse turned to him. "What do you do?"

"I'm sorry?" Rowan stared at her, not sure what she was asking.

"I mean, for a living. What do you do? Don't you have employment?"

Rowan gave a quick grin. "I do have that. I am an artist, doing paintings from photographs or else using photographs to illustrate my books."

"Books? As in?"

"Travel books. A blog. Dad and Mom are involved in the blog and have carried it on. I didn't have any books outstanding when I left." He sighed. "I guess I need to go home."

"But you're not ready yet, are you?" Saoirse stood. "It's starting to get chilly. We need to go in, Rowan." Without thinking she extended her hand, not surprised when he took hers. What surprised her was that he didn't let go of her as they walked back towards the house, not seeing the light from the cigarette being smoked by the man standing in the shadows.

Chapter 12

Saoirse waited at the counter in her father's business, watching Kelly as he paced. That he was upset, she knew, but not just why.

"Dad?" Her voice finally brought him back to the present.

"Saoirse? I didn't know that you were here." Kelly walked towards her, to stand leaning against the counter. "What am I to do with you?"

"Dad? You've lost me. Just what are you talking about?" Saoirse frowned, her eyes on the paper in her father's hand. "And just what is that?" She stabbed a finger at it.

"This?" Kelly stared down at the paper. "I'm waiting for someone from the police to come. I asked for Bill specifically."

"And why?" Saoirse reached for the paper, only to have her father hold it away from her. "Dad?"

"Saoirse? When you were in the garden last night, did you see anyone?" Kelly watched her carefully.

"No. I didn't. Rowan and I were talking but I didn't see anyone else. Why?" She suddenly grew afraid. "Dad? What aren't you saying?"

"That someone was there, watching you. In fact, he was very close to you. There is a patrol vehicle heading that way for the officer to search the area."

Saoirse paled. "Dad? Now what?"

"Now what is that you be more aware of your surroundings, Saoirse." Bill's voice behind her had Saoirse jumping in fright before she spun to face him, a hand held to her throat.

"Bill? I didn't hear you."

"And that's a big problem, Saoirse. You need to be more aware of what's going on around you. We talked about that just last night."

Kelly watched as Saoirse attempted to stare down Bill, a quiet amusement in his eyes as he wondered who would win. His bet was on Bill.

"I know that, Bill. But I have to live. I can't be enclosed or locked up." Saoirse started to brush by him, stopping at his hand on her arm.

"I know that, Saoirse. Believe me, I know that. But if you don't work with us, you might not survive. Are you prepared to put your family and friends through that kind of loss?" Bill was stern and brutally open with Saoirse, knowing that was just how he had to be.

Saoirse paled even more. "Bill?" Her voice was a mere whisper. "Don't!"

"It's the truth, Saoirse, and you know that. We don't have any idea who is after you or even why. We can speculate until the cows come home as my grandfather would have said but until we have more facts or they up the threat factor, we just ask that you be careful." Bill reached out a gloved hand to take the paper from Kelly, his eyes dropping to it. "And this is part of it. They were that close to you last night, Saoirse, that if you had been on your own, we not likely would be having this conversation. You would have disappeared and not be seen again."

Saoirse began to pace, her arms wrapped around herself. Kelly watched her, knowing that Bill was as well. She finally stopped in front of her father, devastation on her face.

"Dad? How do I do this? You need me here. I can't work remotely. And I won't quit." Her voice had a wobble to it by the time she finished.

Kelly sighed and reached to hug her, his prayer for her whispering in her ear.

"I know that, love. I know that. Security is aware of what is going on. Jason will work from in here, he tells me. Rodney and Aaron will work the outside. Jason's bringing in his dog."

"They would do that?"

"They would. Bill?"

"That works. At least for now. It may come to the point that Saoirse can't work from here. Do what you need to for her to work remotely. It may mean her life or death." With that grim warning, Bill walked away, leaving Saoirse devastated as she watched him leave.

Kelly sighed before he turned to head for his office, his mind racing as to just how they would work it with Saoirse. He reached for his phone, a call put to his computer expert. A few questions and it was agreed that Wayne would set up a computer at their home for Saoirse to work from, remotely connecting to the office.

Saoirse stood in her father's office doorway, watching him as he hung up the phone.

"Dad? What did you do?"

"I set it up with Wayne to have you work remotely. That way, you won't have to come in. We can forward the faxes to the home fax and you can work with that. I'll talk to one of the security men and see if they'll run courier for us back and forth between there and here."

Chapter 13

A week had passed since Kelly received that letter. He had not received another one but was on constant alert. Jason had taken to being at the house during the day, his yellow lab, Raider, with him. Saoirse had told him to go back to work but he had just grinned at her and continued moving around the yard. She had watched him, shaking her head, feeling responsible for him being there. And she was, she decided. Her prayer was that whoever it was would be caught and caught quickly. That didn't seem to be happening, was her thought.

That afternoon, she sat at the desk her father had installed in the office for her, working away on quotes and responses to emails. She didn't notice that Rowan had placed a cup of tea beside her before he headed for the easy chair near the fireplace.

She finally looked up, seeing him for the first time as he sat. His head was back on the chair and his eyes closed. Saoirse frowned. *He doesn't look much better, does he, Lord? He still has that fragile, worn-out look. His eyes are still so dull. I know that he is trying but he is beaten down yet and not back to normal. Please, Lord? Heal our friend.* She didn't realize that her features had softened as she watched him, not knowing that he was capturing her heart day by day.

Rowan roused, his head raising as he looked around before he settled back. He had been certain that he had heard one of his captors but that couldn't be, now could it, he thought.

Saoirse had risen, heading for the kitchen, a frown on her face as she stared at the cup she had picked up from the desk. No, she didn't remember bringing that cup with her. She shrugged, watching Connell as he worked away.

"Grilling tonight, Connell?" Her voice had her brother looking around, a grin on his face. "You might as well give up your apartment and move back in too."

"Not happening, sis. I just wanted to do something for Mom and Dad. Mom's been run off her feet with her patients, she tells me. So many sick people right now."

"That there are. You would almost think that we were in the middle of flu season and we're not." She set the cup in the sink and washed her hands. "What can I do?"

"Nothing for me, sis. But Rowan? See if you can get him outside. Mom says that he doesn't go out much."

"I will go do what the doctor ordered. Let me know if you need me."

Connell watched her walk away, a frown on his face as he thought through what his father had told him just an hour before. He had asked Connell to stop by the house, that they needed to all meet and make some decisions. Bill had been around, he told his son and had warned Kelly that there were now rumours on the street that someone was looking for Saoirse. The reason why was not just evident.

Saoirse hesitated before she laid her hand on Rowan's shoulder, rousing him.

"Rowan? Come on outside. We need to be in the fresh air. The sun is shining. The birds are singing. The bees are buzzing and the insects are humming away. The air is laden with the scent of whatever flowers and shrubs are blooming. You need this."

Rowan had stared at her as she spoke before he shook his head.

"Are you sure you're not a poet?" He watched as she grinned at him before he rose, his hand going out to capture hers. "Lead the way, Saoirse. I am sure that you have just the spot that you want to be."

"I do. There is another area in the garden that I love. It's where the coneflowers and daisies are. Daisies are one of my favourite flowers. I need to do some work there." She turned slightly to stare back at her desk. "I need a break from all that. Dad would tell me it's quiting time. And Connell is getting ready to grill our supper."

"I should help him." Rowan turned from the door, ready to head for the kitchen.

"Nope. Outside, buster. Doctor's orders." She stared down at their hands as they walked across the lawn but made no effort to release hers. "Mom wants you outside, she said." She looked up at him, marvelling at how tall he was.

"She does, does she?" A flicker of a grin passed over his face. "Then I must obey." He stopped, his eyes closing as he took a deep breath, listening to the sounds that she had described, breathing in the scents she had mentioned. "Your mother was right. I need this. Mom would have been after me too."

"Where are your parents, anyway?" Saoirse just stood, content she thought to be with him and that was an unusual feeling for her. She usually disappeared if a man showed any interest in her.

"They're away on a planned trip and vacation. I told them to keep their plans. Dad has a business where he travels and then submits his photos and videos to travel agencies."

"That's an interesting line of work." She hesitated. "Are you feeling any better, Rowan?"

He shrugged. "I'm not sure. Physically, I am, but mentally and emotionally? I'm not sure. I'll never be the same man that I was before. Spiritually, I'm struggling. I just don't understand why God allowed me to be held captive."

"That's a good question, Rowan." Saoirse dropped to her knees near the flowerbed, her hands reaching for the weeds. Rowan dropped to a sitting position beside her.

"It is. I used to read articles about that happening to people and wondered how they coped. I coped by shutting down. I just can't seem to find my way back."

"You will. I am confident of that. God is working in your life. Maybe you can use your experience in the future to help others. Who knows what His plans are for you." She leaned back on her hands. "I often wonder why we go through what we do."

———

48

"I agree with you." Rowan rolled a blade of grass between his fingers, his eyes on the horizon. "Being here with your family has helped, I think. Your mom is looking after my physical health. Your father is looking after my spiritual health. Connell challenges me to get up and get moving every day." He gave a small grin. "Did you know that he texts me every morning with a Scripture verse and a challenge for the day?"

"He does? That doesn't surprise me. I get a verse every day as well." Saoirse waited for him to continue but when he didn't, she just had to ask. "You didn't say what I do for you. Or am I not to ask?"

Rowan turned to her, his hand reaching for her braid, running down it before he pulled off the tie, loosening the hair. "You have such beautiful hair. Why keep it back?"

"Because as much as I like it long, it can get in my way." She stared at him, a puzzled look in her eyes.

"Leave it loose. It suits you." He watched her closely. "And you? What do you do for me?"

Saoirse nodded. "Yes. What do I do for you? I'm curious."

"And you do remember that curiosity killed the cat."

"But satisfaction brought it back. Please?"

Rowan sighed, not quite sure how to phrase what he wanted to say. "You? Saoirse, you have no idea what you do for me. I am told that I went there to find you and protect you. You are my reason for getting up in the morning, for getting through the day, for trying to find my way back to reality. If circumstances had been different and we had met, I would probably have asked you out on a date. You are a beautiful, talented, loving lady. You challenge me to get better, to get back to where I was or to where I need to be."

"I do that?" Saoirse was surprised. "I didn't know that." Then her eyes narrowed. "A date? Really?"

"Really, Saoirse. You are now an important part of my life and I don't want to lose that." He looked past her to where Connell was approaching. "Your brother is heading this way."

—

"So?" She sighed, her body slumping somewhat. "Okay. Conversation over. For now." She was on her feet, moving towards the house.

Connell dropped down to where she had been sitting, his eyes on his friend.

"Rowan?"

"Connell?" Rowan refused to be baited.

"If you hurt her, you answer to me." Connell was playing the big brother and both the men knew that.

"I promise. I will do my best not to." Rowan was on his feet, walking rapidly after Saoirse, catching up with her, his hand reaching for hers.

Connell watched, a sigh coming from him. *They're falling in love, aren't they, Lord? And I am so afraid for my sister.*

Chapter 14

Two days later, Saoirse sat at her desk, terror coursing through her. Her eyes were glued to the letter that she had just unfolded. Her hands were shaking hard enough that the paper was rattling. Rowan looked up from the book that he had been trying to read. With a soft exclamation, he was on his feet and beside her. His hands gently removed the paper from hers and then drew her up and away from the desk, through the French doors to the outside. Ruth took one look and then ran for her phone, calling Kelly and then Bill.

Rowan swept an arm around Saoirse, turning her into his shoulder, his other hand up in a stop motion as Ruth approached. The question on her face had him shaking his head.

"A letter I think, Ruth. She had the paper in her hand." Rowan's voice was low, but Saoirse still raised her head.

Saoirse made no effort to move away from Rowan, finding the comfort that she needed. She sat as he shoved her down, his arm still around her. Ruth was there, bending over her daughter, the doctor in her reaching for her wrist.

"Mom? Aren't you working?" Saoirse was disoriented for the moment.

"No, not today, dear. It's Saturday. And you should not have been working either."

"I know, Mom, but I had to do something. This is really getting to me. Not having any freedom."

"We know, but from now on, you only work the hours that you would at the office. No more than that." Ruth pulled over a chair. "What happened?"

Her daughter's face whitened even more, scaring Ruth herself. Saoirse simply shook her head.

"Is Bill coming?"

"He is. And I think Andrew as well. They were at lunch, Bill said. Dad can't. He's in a conference call with a mission."

Bill and Andrew shared a look before they approached, Rowan rising and coming towards them. Bill frowned, seeing the clearing eyes of the other man, and the anger in them.

"Rowan?"

Rowan pointed to the house. "In there. She had a paper in her hand."

Bill nodded, heading for the house. Andrew waited, his eyes on Saoirse before Ruth rose and headed for him.

"Andrew?"

Andrew kept his eyes on Saoirse before he spoke. "Can you go with Bill, Ruth? See what he needs. Rowan, back with Saoirse." Andrew's eyes raised, searching the area. "We need to get you two inside and now."

Rowan stared at him startled before his hand reached for Saoirse's to draw her to her feet. He headed for the sunroom before Andrew's voice stopped him.

"Not the sunroom, Rowan. The kitchen. Bill will need time to assess whatever it is Saoirse saw."

Rowan nodded, heading for that door, finding Kelly heading his way.

"Rowan? What is going on? I got Ruth's message that I needed to come home."

"Saoirse opened a letter, I gather." Andrew's hand on Kelly's arm stopped his movement. "Bill is in the office now, looking at whatever it is. We were having lunch and I just came along with him. Ruth is there." Andrew nodded towards the kitchen door. "Your daughter needs you."

"I know. I was hoping it was over." Kelly ran his hand through his graying hair. "I guess it's not."

"No. It's not. And I can see Saoirse running, just to protect you three."

"She will. And there won't be a thing that we can do to stop her. And she won't let us go along." He paused before he shook his head, not expressing the thought that he had.

"And Rowan will try and stop her or go along. Is that your thought?" Andrew gave a grim smile. "I can see him doing that. I am surprised that she hasn't run yet."

Kelly shot him a look. "You thought that she would have?"

Andrew held the kitchen door, his eyes on the young couple inside. Rowan sat with his arm around Saoirse, who had her head buried in her folded arms, her body shaking with the suppressed sobs that she refused to shed.

Bill and Andrew finally left, Bill's words of caution causing Saoirse just to stare at him. He exchanged a glance with Andrew who shrugged. They had done what they could. It was now up to Saoirse to follow their suggestions or not. They could not force her to.

"Saoirse, what was in the letter?" Kelly sat beside his daughter, his hand on hers.

"I can't. Dad, I just can't. They threatened all of you. How do I find what they want and make them leave me alone?"

Kelly's heart broke for his daughter, seeing the tears gathered in her eyes.

"It won't matter, love. They will still come after you, even if you gave them what they wanted. They won't stop. Not anymore." He frowned. "From what Bill said, they are not just asking for whatever it is that they think you have."

"No. They weren't. I don't get it, Dad. I just don't get it."

Chapter 15

Dressed and with his small backpack at his feet, Rowan stood on the back deck early the next morning. It was early enough that it was still dark, the moon just finding the horizon. He had watched Saoirse carefully the night before and then made a decision. He knew that she was going to run and he would not let her run on her own. His mind had cleared that suddenly the day before when he realized how much danger she was in. He didn't understand that it was because the lady he was learning to love was in danger and he felt a need to protect her.

Saoirse closed the kitchen door quietly behind her, a quick indrawn breath the only giveaway of how she felt. She jumped, a hand covering her mouth when Rowan's hand found her.

"Rowan?" Her voice hissed at him in a quiet whisper.

"Wherever you're running to, I'm running with you. I can't let you go on your own." Rowan stood in her way until she nodded. "Okay. So where are we off to?"

Saoirse stared at him before she headed down the steps and towards the back of the yard.

"The bus station. I'm heading out of town." She pulled the baseball cap on her head down further. "You need a cap or something."

"I'll buy one at the station. Where are we heading out of town?"

Settling into a seat at the back of the bus, Saoirse stared out of the window, sadness in her gaze. She had no idea when she would be back. She had left a note for her parents but she knew that her father would be looking for her. *Please, Lord? Keep them and Connell safe. I couldn't handle it if something happened to them.* She felt the pressure from Rowan's hand as he held hers, something that he had been doing that morning.

Rowan's heart raised in prayer for his lady. He had no idea what they were facing but one thing he knew. It wasn't right that they were running together like this. Not as singles. He sighed once more, something that he felt he had been doing a lot the last few days.

"Where in Oak City are you heading?"

Saoirse turned her attention to him. "I'm looking for Phoebe's cousin. Or sort of cousin. It's a long story, but she was stolen as a child and raised thinking the police chief was her cousin. I've met him on numerous occasions. He'll help us." She settled down into her seat, her head on his shoulder. "You didn't have to come. In fact, you shouldn't have."

"I know, Saoirse, but I had to." He bit at his lip. "How long do you plan on being gone?" He felt her shrug. "That long? Then we need to talk. We can't roam around on our own, not like this."

She raised her head to stare at him before it went back down on his shoulder.

"We can't?"

"No, we can't. We have two choices. Either we go home or ....." His voice died away.

When he didn't continue, Saoirse tilted her head to watch his face, seeing the distress and conflict on his.

"Rowan?"

"We can't roam around as two singles, Saoirse. That would destroy your reputation. As I said, we return home or we marry." He drew a deep breath, not quite sure that he should have said what he did.

Saoirse tugged at her hand, finding that she could not release it from Rowan's strong grasp. She stared at their hands, thinking that he had regained his strength.

"Did you really just say that?" Her words were almost hissed at him.

"I did. Either we go home or we marry. And don't even suggest that I leave you on your own. That's not happening." His words had a strong bite of anger in them when he finished.

"We need to talk then, don't we?" Saoirse turned her head to stare out the window, blinking rapidly at the tears. This was not how she ever expected to receive a proposal but she had to admit that she knew what he was saying. That had been tugging at her, them wandering around as she had planned. "I don't know, Rowan. Is it God's will that we do this?"

"We pray about it on our way to Oak City. Then we find somewhere to have our breakfast while we make plans." His finger hit her lips, stilling her words. "No, we pray, Saoirse. If either of us still has hesitation, then we board a bus back to Elmton."

Chapter 16

Their steps matching as they walked away from the bus station, Rowan and Saoirse didn't speak. They had pulled their caps down further over their eyes and shouldered their packs. Her hand was tight in his. Saoirse's face held her emotions as she was unable to control them. Rowan's face was grim but shuttered. Neither saw the man who had been leaning against a storefront across from the station straighten up and then begin following them.

Setting down his coffee cup, Rowan stared out of the window in the diner that they had selected. He didn't feel safe and he had no idea why. He turned his head to search the room, frowning at the man who sat facing them. The man's head was down but Rowan was certain that he was watching them. He sighed to himself, something he thought that he had been doing on a regular basis.

"Rowan?" Saoirse's quiet voice drew his eyes to her. He heard the wobble at the end of his name, a wobble that she was trying hard to control.

"Saoirse? Are you sure that you want to run?" He waited, compassion in his gaze, but something else that drew her eyes to his.

"I don't know anymore, Rowan. I just don't know. I thought I was doing the right thing." She felt her phone vibrating and pulled it out, unlocking it. She stared down at it. "Dad."

Rowan was on his feet, sliding in beside her, his hand reaching to answer the call but not saying anything, shaking his head at Saoirse as she opened her mouth.

"Saoirse? I know that you are there. I can tell that you have answered. It's okay, love. We know why you ran. It's not what we would have wanted you to do, but we do understand. If Rowan is with you, that's good. He'll keep you safe. Just keep in touch, love. That's all we ask. A text message. A voice mail. Let us know that you are well. I won't stay on the line, love, but we love you both. You have our prayers." Kelly's voice dropped for a moment as he struggled to control his emotions. "Connell is watching for you to come home. Don't. Not yet. Bill has been around this morning. He's to try and call you. At least speak with him." The call cut off. Kelly wiped at his eyes as he turned his phone over and over on the desk.

Rowan's hand found Saoirse as he prayed for her and her family. He finally looked up, staring out of the window, biting at his lip. Uncertainty was in his mind and heart. He was not sure that they were making the right decision.

"Rowan? What now?" Saoirse leaned against him, drawing from his strength. "You're still not well enough to be on the run for long."

"It's you that I am worried about. How do we do this?"

"I don't want us to marry. Not like this. But we can't continue to run." Saoirse stared out the window as well. "I am so torn, Rowan. Maybe this was all a mistake. Maybe we should just go home."

"We can do that. Or I can take you to my home and we can make a decision there."

She turned to him. "I'm not sure where your home is."

He gave a brief grin that lit up his face. "It's here, Saoirse. Here is Oak City. You didn't know that?"

She shook her head and then reached for her backpack. They had already paid for their meal.

"We need to move, Rowan. How far to your place?"

"A ways. There's a bus that stops outside." He glanced out the window, stood and reached for his own backpack. "In fact, I see it coming now. Let's run."

Saoirse wandered Rowan's home, hearing him in the kitchen making coffee and tea for them and then found him right behind her.

———

58

"Saoirse?" Rowan was puzzled, not sure what she was thinking.

"You have a nice place here. Why would you ever leave it to go and find me?"

"Because you are the daughter of a dear friend of my father. And secondly, there is no way that I could not act, not when a lady was in trouble." He simply reached to hug her. "I need to check on my emails and see what is happening." He pointed to the television. "It works if you want it to."

Saoirse gave a brief laugh, catching the fun in his eyes. "Thank you, Rowan. I just might."

Rowan headed for his office, finding it strange to be home after what five months or more? It doesn't feel like home anymore, does it, Lord? I think I could move to Elmton very easily. Guide my decisions. Protect my lady, please, dear Lord? I sense that we are only beginning with what is happening with her.

Immersed in his emails, he vaguely heard the sound of the television as Saoirse turned it on. He smiled. He could get used to this, he thought, before he was on his feet, running for the living room as Saoirse screamed.

"Saoirse?" He searched for someone there and found no one. When he turned back to her, he found her pointing at the television.

"Our garage!"

"What?" Rowan turned to the television as well, shock on his face as he saw the fire engulfing the garage. "You're sure?"

"I am. Oh, Rowan! What did I do?"

"I don't know that you did anything wrong."

They listened as the news reporter described the scene, noting that no one had been home at the time. They watched as he tried to elicit information from the investigators and was ignored.

Saoirse reached for her phone as it vibrated.

"It's Bill." She answered, not saying anything once more.

"Saoirse? I know that you're there. This is a warning, do you understand that?" Bill's voice was grim. "We're putting your parents somewhere safe. Connell is working the fire and will stay working. He doesn't feel that he can leave. This, Saoirse? This is why we didn't want you to run. They'll keep doing this, finding people that you are close to and threatening them. I know you're there. Call me."

Chapter 17

Saoirse roused a couple of hours later. She had not even been aware that she had drifted off to sleep, held tight against Rowan as they sat together on the couch. This had worn her out, she thought. How do I go on, Lord? How do I do this? I know that life and death are part of what we face, the chain of life as some call it. I just don't want to be responsible for anyone's death.

A sudden thought had Saoirse on her feet, looking for Rowan. She hesitated at his office doorway, watching him.

Rowan looked up at the whisper of noise that Saoirse made and was on her feet, his hands reaching for hers.

"Have a good nap?"

She shrugged. "I guess. I didn't realize that I had slept." She paused, a frown puckering her brow. "I had a thought, Rowan, and I'm not sure how to investigate it."

"And that would be?" Rowan drew her to his desk, gently shoving her down into his chair before he reached for another one.

"The last time I went out on the mission, about six or seven months ago, we were to bring back someone with us. She had been working at the mission and was due to be furloughed. But she was killed before we could leave. She was about my age, not from this area. We brought her body home." She closed her eyes, a tear tracing down her cheek. "The father didn't take it well. He thought that we should have kept her safe."

"And it wasn't your responsibility, was it?" She shook her head. "Then, he's blaming the wrong people."

"I guess." Saoirse stared at the monitor. "We were responsible for bringing her home. We had taken down a load of equipment and medical supplies. The agreement to bring her home was a last-minute one if I remember correctly."

"And whoever killed her would have known this?"

"Maybe." Saoirse sighed. "We were using the cargo plane and only had room for the few that went with us and her."

"And you think the father might be behind this?"

Saoirse shrugged. "I have no idea. I don't know that Dad even knew all the details. Connell does." She reached for her phone. "Connell needs to talk to Bill and tell him." She sent off a swift text, surprised to find Connell responding just as quickly. "Oh, good. He has. And now Bill will want to talk to me again. It doesn't end."

"No, it doesn't. But just maybe we can find the end of this soon." Rowan looked around. "I think I'll move to Elmton. I want a smaller town."

"You will? I'm surprised."

"I'm not. There is a beautiful lady that I would like to get to know better, you know, date, go on walks with her, just sit and talk. And she lives there."

She stared at him. "You would do that? Move from here to there? You could do that?"

"I could. Before all this happened, I was thinking of moving somewhere else. I would like a smaller town."

"Elmton is small. It's a nice town." She sighed as she looked at the computer monitor. "I need to search something but I'm not sure how to."

"What is it that you feel you need to research?"

Saoirse shrugged. "I have no idea. I was thinking of that lady. She's around my age." She paled. "She looked something like me, only her hair was just brown and short. Her eyes were brown. So there is no way that I would be mistaken for her."

"No. Not likely." Rowan reached for his phone. "It's Bill. Sending a text. He wants to speak with you and now, Saoirse." He dialled Bill's number, putting the phone on speaker so that Saoirse could hear as well.

"Buckley." Bill sounded distracted.

"Bill? It's Rowan."

"Rowan!" Bill drew out Rowan's name. "So nice of you to call. Where are you two?"

"Safe for now. You called?"

"I did. I have a question for Saoirse. I know that she's with you. Saoirse. Connell sent me a name. What about that?"

"She was to come back from that last mission trip when we took stuff down there. She was killed before she could come home. Her father was not happy with us. He thought we would protect her. That wasn't our position. We were merely transporting equipment and supplies. And we never left the site the three days we were there, other than for the pilot. He stayed with the plane." Saoirse could barely finish, she was that upset.

"I see. Connell gave me the names. I will be looking into that to see if it has anything to do with this. You need to come home, you two. Running won't help."

Rowan clicked off his phone, cutting off Bill's words.

"Rowan!" Saoirse stared at him. "You just hung up on Bill."

"I know. I don't want to keep the connection open for too long. You don't know who might be listening in. I have to have my phone checked out. Someone could have put on a tracking program when I was held captive."

Saoirse paled. "And they would know exactly where you are, right now. Turn off your phone. Please?"

Rowan did that, then reached to shut down his computer. "I'll have Dad pack up for me. All I need to take is my laptop. That will fit into my pack." He turned as he heard a noise at the front door and moved quickly that way, standing to watch out the window.

"Saoirse, quick. Your pack. We need to move from here and now."

The pair ran for the back door, Rowan pulling it closed and locking it before he pointed towards the attached garage and the gate that led to the neighbour's yard. They were through it and heading for the next yard before the man at the door had even walked to the backyard.

Chapter 18

Saoirse finally dropped to the ground, her back against the brick wall of the building Rowan had led her to. He stood at the corner, watching the way that they had just fled from. He finally turned to drop beside her, his arms resting on his upraised knees, his head dropping from fatigue.

"Rowan? What was that about?"

"Someone was at the door. I didn't know him. I don't think he had our health and welfare in mind."

"Oh! You could have told me."

"I didn't think that I had time to do that." He pulled out his phone, starting it up again, and then scrolling through his messages. "Dad was called when the security company couldn't raise me. Whoever it was broke in." He grew sad. "Dad says he trashed the place. And just where am I?"

"We need to go back, Rowan. We can't run. It will end up with someone getting hurt or worse killed."

"I know." Rowan sent off a swift message to his father and then closed his phone. "Dad will pick me up another phone to use while we have this one looked at. He has a friend who has a security team that will do that."

"Who don't you know?" Saoirse didn't mean to be sarcastic.

"Sarcasm, sweetheart? Richard goes to our church. He knows Andrew and Bill."

"Who don't they know?" Saoirse dropped her head back to rest on the wall. "Where do we meet your Dad?"

"At dark and at the diner near the bus stop. We'll have to put in a few hours."

"I know. Where do we go then?"

Rowan was on his feet, his hand reaching for hers, not letting it drop when she stood.

"I say we go to city hall, get our license and then make a decision. We don't have to use it today."

Saoirse stared at him. "You're still serious about that?"

"I am. And I have no idea why. I mean, we don't know each other that well." He stared at Saoirse as she began to laugh. "What did I say?"

"Have you ever talked to Andrew about him and Phoebe?" When he shook his head, she laughed again. "Andrew was asked to go into some roadhouse and rescue her. She couldn't talk at that point as she had shut down. They married the next day, thinking it was the only way to keep Phoebe alive. You know how much in love they are."

"They are. I didn't know their history. I would never have guessed."

"No, you wouldn't have. Silas and Madigan married to save each other's lives. Bill and Cora had been married before, each to someone else but reunited here in town. They were high school sweethearts."

Rowan rose, pulling Saoirse to her feet. "We need to keep moving, I think, sweetheart. Let's head for somewhere we can sit for a while and grab a bite to eat."

"Is that all you think of?" Saoirse was grumbling and they both knew that.

"Hey! I've been sick. I need to regain my strength." He grinned at her as he stopped at a street vendor and purchased burgers and a drink for them.

"Fast food?" Saoirse was not a fan of fast food, never had been.

"It is what it is, Saoirse. I know. It's fast food. I'm not crazy about it myself but for once, we eat it and be happy." He pointed towards a park bench. "There, I think. We can see anyone coming at us and I know the area. We can get away from there without too much trouble.”

Just as dusk was falling, Ronan watched the pair trudge towards him. *Lord, they're tired. How do we help them? Rowan won't want to let Saoirse go anywhere on her own. That much Kelly has expressed to me. Is she his lady? The lady Lydia wove into his bedtime stories when he was young? Is that why he had to rescue her? That he believed knights always rescued ladies in trouble? Please, Lord, protect my son.*

Rowan opened the back door of the car, almost shoved Saoirse inside and then slid in himself, the door closing quietly after him. He nodded at the question on his father's face.

“Dad? Thanks.”

“Never a problem. Now, where would you two like to run to?” Ronan twisted so that he could watch them.

“Home, I think, Dad. Your home. Mine's a crime scene right now.”

“It is? That's not something that you shared with me.” Ronan turned to face the front, starting the car and driving away. “I wasn't aware that you knew. The security company called me when they couldn't reach you.”

“No, I didn't get a chance. Someone broke in and we had to flee.” Rowan searched the area as his father drove away. “There. There's someone coming after us. He's on foot though, Dad.”

“I'm sure that our place is being watched.” Ronan drove in a circuitous manner, finally heading for his home. “Duck down, you two, until I pull into the garage.”

Lydia looked around as the trio entered before she was hugging her son, holding on a little bit tighter and longer than she normally would. She stared at Saoirse before she just swept her into a tight hug.

“Mom. Dad. We're in danger. And we have likely brought that danger here.” Rowan paced, a hand rubbing at his cheek.

—

"We are aware of that, son." Ronan stopped Rowan with a hand to his arm. "I spoke with Andrew and then Bill. Kelly has also called. They all seemed to think that you would call me."

"Which I did. If they guessed that, others will." Rowan was troubled.

Saoirse shook her head. "We need to leave, Ronan. Lydia. We can't put you at risk."

"No, you can't but you're here and will stay the night." Lydia pointed to the hall. "Rowan, your room is ready. Show Saoirse the spare room. Get cleaned up. By that time, I'll have supper on the table."

Chapter 19

The next morning, Rowan sat on the side of his bed, rubbing at his face. He frowned. He needed a shower and shave but just didn't know if he had the energy to do that. He forced himself to his feet and found clean clothes.

Showered, shaved, and in clean clothes, Rowan headed for the kitchen. He paused as the open door to the spare room and then began to panic. *She's run,* he thought, *and left me behind.* He slid to a halt as he entered the kitchen, finding Saoirse sitting at the table, a woebegone look on her face.

"Saoirse?" Rowan was in a chair beside her, his arm around her.

"Rowan? Can we go home?" She shoved her phone at him.

"What's wrong?" He stared at her and then took the phone that she kept shoving at him. "What's this?"

"This? It's a bomb threat. At our home. I need to see my mom and dad."

"Let me call Bill."

"I already did. He said we should stay away. That this was to try and bring me back home." Tears covered her cheeks.

Rowan hugged her tight even as he heard his mother and father moving around them. He shook his head at his father.

"We can go there. I'll take you. You need to see them."

Saoirse nodded. "But what if Bill is right? That this is to draw me out? I can't bring harm to them."

Ronan sat beside her, his hand reaching for hers. He prayed for her, his prayer calming her heart.

"How be I call Richard? See if he can take you back there? He's said he'll do what he can to help."

"You would do that?" Saoirse stared at him, her lips trembling as she fought her emotions.

"I would, Saoirse. You are a member of our family, whether you realize it or not. Your father was a good friend of mine. I am sorry that we lost touch. He went in and saved my son. I can do no less for his daughter." Ronan was on his feet, his phone out as he headed for his office.

Lydia took his place, her hands reaching for Saoirse as she too prayed for her.

"Richard will assess the risk, Saoirse, and then make a decision based on that. He will not go if he feels you would be at too much risk."

Richard stood at the entrance to the living room two hours later, his eyes on Rowan. He shook his head. He's in love, isn't he, Lord? And not quite sure how to proceed. That's not like him. He's usually so confident. But then going through what he did? That shakes him. Shakes his faith in You, Lord. Restore him.

Rowan looked up and then was on his feet, his hand out to shake Richard's.

"Richard. Thanks for coming. This is Saoirse."

Richard shook her hand and then seated himself near them, his eyes assessing them both. He watched with a tinge of amusement as Saoirse kept herself as close to Rowan as she could.

"Richard? What news?" Rowan finally spoke for the two of them.

"Rowan. Saoirse. I have spoken with Bill and Andrew. They are of a mind that you now need to come back home. Bill needs you available to speak with him when he needs to. He can't do that if you are on the run." Richard's voice was stern yet kindly.

"I know that. I just wasn't thinking of anything other than keeping Mom and Dad and Connell safe. I wasn't trusting God as I should have been." Saoirse wiped at her face, angry with herself for crying. She jumped as a large white handkerchief appeared in her vision.

"Use it, Saoirse." Richard's voice startled her. "We'll talk. I know of somewhere I can put you two but you would be under our watch. I'm not sure that you're ready to do that."

Saoirse shook her head. "I can't. And I can't let Rowan do that. It would be too much like his captivity."

Richard nodded, watching Rowan as he did so. He shook his head once more. Rowan, you want to protect her but you're not sure how to or even if she will let you.

"We'll head out in about an hour or so. Paul and Silver will be with us. I don't need the whole team." He was on his feet. "I'll be back in an hour. Be ready to move."

Saoirse stared after him, her mouth open until a gentle tap under her chin with Rowan's finger closed it.

"Did he just do that?"

"He did, Saoirse. He thinks far ahead of where he is. If he says to be ready, we need to be ready. I have no idea where he'll take us, but I am sure that you'll see your parents and brother." Rowan watched her. "What can I do for you?"

She shrugged, the woebegone look back as she twisted the handkerchief in her hands. "I never gave this back."

"That's okay. You can when Richard returns. He'll have some instructions for us." Rowan was on his feet, pulling her up and then with him to the office. "Do you need to check emails or anything like that?"

Saoirse shook her head. "No, I put a vacation response on them so I don't have to." She bit at her lip. "How do we do this, Rowan?" Her eyes sought his, a frown on her face at the look in his eyes. A look that said she was beautiful and that he wanted her in his life.

Rowan shook his head. "We'll let Richard direct us. Let's spend some time in prayer, sweetheart. We will need it."

Saoirse frowned at him harder, her heart grasping at what he had called her but her mind not sure if he had even meant it.

—

Chapter 20

Staring past Rowan as he sat beside her in Richard's SUV, Saoirse watched the scenery flying by outside the vehicle. She was glad it was but so afraid for her family. Was she bringing harm to them? *This is so hard, Lord. I need to trust You. I need to cling to You as my anchor right now but I can't. I just don't have it in me. Help me, dear Lord.*

Silver watched the couple carefully before she nodded. *Another couple in love,* she thought, *and that scares both of them. They are taking baby steps towards one another but both are so afraid of what is happening to them. Lord, You need to take control. Is this the chain of life stuff that Paul is always talking about? Life and love and death? I suspect it is. They are not sure of where to head either, are they, Lord? Help us to help them.*

Richard had twisted slightly in the passenger's seat to study them before he shared a look with Paul, who was the driver. Paul shook his head slightly. They had at least one car following them. That much he knew. He was sure that there were others. Word would get out that they were heading home.

"Richard?" Rowan's voice finally broke the silence. "Where are we heading?"

"To Saoirse's parents. They are home for now. Don and his crew are there until we figure out what to do." Richard caught the puzzled look on Saoirse's face. "Don is a friend and has a security team as well. And we have another friend who would step in if needed."

"I wish this had never happened. This is putting everyone at risk." Saoirse wiped at the tears on her cheeks. "I hate this. I never cry."

Silver reached to hug her. "It's okay, Saoirse. Sometimes our emotions just take over. We can't control that. I always find a good cry helps."

"You do?" Paul grinned at her as he turned his head for a brief moment.

"Yes, I do. You've seen me cry." Silver shook her finger at him. "Saoirse, did Richard explain what happens now?"

"He did, but I just don't understand. Why are we heading for Mom and Dad? Should we not stay apart from one another?"

Richard twisted to watch her. "For now, we need you all together. Your brother is working, Bill says, and he'll be with his teammates for now. Bill says that a fellow officer has volunteered to stay with him when he's off duty."

"Oh! I didn't know that!" Saoirse shook for a moment. "This is so horrible. Who is after me? Or are they after Rowan?"

"Bill is working on that premise as well." Richard shared a look with Rowan. "If Rowan had not gone down there, who knows how he would have become involved. But because he did, that put him on their radar. Our question is this. Who knew his relationship to your family, Saoirse, and who knew that he was heading down there to find you?"

Saoirse paled. "I have no idea. Rowan, how long after I left did you go down?"

Rowan shrugged. "I think I headed down there just before you came back. A day or so before? I never did make it to the mission." His mind turned back to those few days. "The only one that I told was Dad and that was just before I boarded the plane. I was in a coffee shop for my lunch just a day or so before that and heard them talking about Kelly, his plane and then Saoirse." He paled. "They mentioned something about artifacts and that Saoirse was the one who would have them. What did I do?"

Richard shook his head. "You didn't do anything except step in to try and help someone. Do you think that you would recognize the men?"

Rowan shook his head. "I didn't see them. They were in a booth behind me. I was reading and then heard Kelly's name. I knew of him from Dad. Then they went on to describe Saoirse and how they needed to find her and keep her with them until they could recover the parcels. But I don't understand. Who placed them?"

"That's something that Bill is working on, I think he indicated." Richard faced forward, his eyes on the approaching city. "Just a few words on how we will proceed. Paul will drive up to your parents' home, Saoirse. You will wait in the vehicle with Silver while Paul and I do a surveillance on the perimeter and the immediate area around the house. Silver will be behind the wheel and if anything is off or we have concerns, she disappears with you two."

Paul's sudden exclamation had Richard's head spinning his way before he too gave an exclamation.

"Brace yourselves!" His words were barely out before Paul's sudden spin of the wheel sent the SUV flying off the road, bouncing through the ditch and then heading for a row of trees. He found desperately to turn it or to even be able to control it without any luck. The vehicle slammed sideways into the trees, Richard's body hitting hard against the door as the vehicle crumpled on his side.

Dust swirled in the air as the vehicle settled back on the four tires. There was silence in the air, not one person moving. None of the vehicle occupants saw the large truck slide to an abrupt stop on the road or see the motorhome that had been following them stop as well.

Chapter 21

The doors of the truck flew open and the men ran for Richard's SUV. They peered in through the windows before the back door was pried open. Rowan was hauled out, his feet not moving properly. A tight hand on his arm guided him towards the motorhome, his feet twisting and stumbling over one another as he tried to stay upright. His head spun from the shock of the accident and his eyes could barely stay open. Rowan was roughly shoved inside and to the floor, where he lay, unmoving.

The second man reached to slice through the seatbelt holding Saoirse in place. He gathered her into his arms, a quick look at the other three occupants before he ran for the motorhome, entering it to dump her limp body on the bed. Her head had dropped backwards over his arm, her free arm and braid swinging with the motion of his rapid steps. He stared at Rowan for a moment before he was off with his partner, the truck heading away from the accident as quickly as it could.

The heavyset man stood watching the SUV before he gave an evil grin and shrugged his jacket into place. The cigar that he had held in his hand was dropped to the ground as he turned to enter the motorhome. He stood for a moment staring down at Rowan, whose head was turning restlessly on the floor. He then stood over Saoirse watching her closely before he shrugged and headed for his seat at the front of the vehicle.

"Head for the farm, Oscar." He stared dispassionately back at the SUV before he reached for his phone. A text message was sent and then he pocketed the phone and sat back.

An hour later, a patrol vehicle happened by, the officer's eyes narrowing as he caught a glimpse of the vehicle in his headlights as dusk dropped down. The large beam from his flashlight lit up the area as he walked towards the SUV, his eyes searching around it. He had heard no report of an accident in this area and there was enough traffic that there should have been.

His light flashed through the windows and then he was reaching for his radio, calling for assistance. He tugged at Paul's door, finally prying it open, a hand reaching for his wrist and then across him to Richard. He pulled open the door to the backseat, repeating his motions with Silver.

The garish red and blue flashes of the emergency lights lit up the night sky a short while later. Andrew stood and watched as the three were removed from the vehicle and taken across the grass to the waiting ambulances. Paul had roused enough to say that he had been boxed in and then run off the road. And he questioned how the others were. He was out again before anyone could respond.

Bill approached Andrew, shrugging up the collar of his jacket against the cool night breeze.

"Just Richard and his two?"

"That's right, Bill." Andrew ducked his head to look into the backseat. "The other two seatbelts had been sliced apart. I would suspect that was done to remove Rowan and Saoirse."

"I would think so. I'll stay if you want to head into the hospital."

"Thanks. I will. You'll need to go and find Kelly and Ruth. Connell was around here but his crew have left. I didn't get a chance to speak with him so I don't know if he is aware that Saoirse was in this vehicle."

"He wouldn't have left if he had known. Not until he spoke with us, knowing that we were here." Bill sighed. "Now where do we do? This was not what we had planned."

Andrew gave a grim smile. "It never is, Bill. We both know that by experience."

Pacing into the emergency room, Andrew searched for Richard, finding him still unconscious. He paused before he approached the physician.

"Doc?"

"Andrew? I didn't expect you to be here." The physician looked between Andrew and Richard.

"He's a friend, Doc, as well as an associate. How is he?"

The physician shrugged. "Lucky to be alive, I would gather. He's hurting, Andrew. His shoulder is messed up. Torn ligaments just for starters. The orthopaedic surgeon is on his way in."

Andrew nodded. "Now, about Paul and Silver?"

"The other two? Paul got off the best. A concussion. Some cuts from where he hit the wheel. And I would like to know why the airbags didn't go off."

"So would I. Silver?"

"She's hurting as well. Bumps. Bruises. A broken arm." The physician walked away. It was a busy day in the Emergency Room and he had other patients to see.

Andrew watched him leave before he approached the stretcher that held Richard. A prayer was raised for his friend before he prayed for Rowan and Saoirse. *We have no idea where they are now, Lord, but You do. Please, dear Lord, protect them? Bring them home and soon.*

Richard's head turned as he roused, pain evident on his face. He squinted as he looked around, not sure exactly where he was.

"Richard? You awake?"

Richard's head turned abruptly, causing him to close his eyes against the pain.

"Andrew? Just where am I?"

"In our hospital. What happened?" Andrew's hands grasped the side rail of the bed, his fingers white from his tight grip.

"I don't remember. I can remember yesterday, I think. I was out with the team doing training, but I don't know what happened today. Was it just today?"

"It was. You were heading this way with Rowan and Saoirse. They are nowhere to be found. Paul and Silver are here in the Emergency Department as well."

Richard raised his head and then tried to sit up, falling back against the bed as his hand sought his shoulder. "What did I do?"

"Your vehicle slammed into a tree. Paul, Silver and you are here. There are no signs of Rowan and Saoirse."

"Rowan I know but who is Saoirse?" Richard's eyes remained closed, his mind not able to comprehend what Andrew had said.

Andrew opened his mouth to reply and then snapped it shut. *Richard, you're not going to be doing much for a while, not with that injury. Heal him, please, dear Lord.*

Chapter 22

Pacing his home office, Kelly kept glancing at either his watch or the clock on the fireplace mantle. *Richard was late,* he thought. *Two hours late.* And he was beginning to worry. This didn't seem to be the character of the man, he decided. *He at least would have called, would he not? Lord? I have no idea what is going on but You do. You want us to trust our children to Your care. It's hard to do just that,* he prayed. *Give us that ability and peace to do just that.*

Ruth walked into his open arms, her own hugging her husband. She blinked back tears of worry and fear.

"Where are they, Kelly? Andrew said that they would be here before now."

"I know. Unless they had to detour or were delayed." Kelly's phone was out, his finger poised over Andrew's number. "I'll call him." He was frustrated when the call went right to voice mail. "Andrew? It's Kelly. Any word on Richard and when he will arrive?"

Connell stood for a moment watching his parents.

"Mom? Dad? Where's Saoirse?" He had entered through the kitchen as was his normal passage of entry. "I didn't see her or Rowan."

"No, neither are here. And I only get Andrew's voice mail. Let me try Bill." Kelly was frustrated again as he only got Bill's voice mail. "Voice mail. Now, where are they?"

Connell stared at his father, his face suddenly paling. "There was an accident outside of town. We were called to it. Two males. One female. They were trapped in an SUV against a tree." Connell's head went back even as his eyes slid closed and a tight, tense look covered his face. "Please, Lord? Not that." He was away from his parents and they heard the door slamming behind him.

Kelly and Ruth exchanged puzzled glances before Kelly was to the front door and outside, his upraised hand to stop his son too late to do that. Ruth stood beside him.

"What is going on?" Her voice was puzzled.

"I have no idea. Unless?" Kelly reached for the door, pulling it closed and locking it. "Come on, Ruth. We're heading for the hospital. I just pray that Saoirse is there. Connell must have realized something and not told us."

Ruth's hand stopped him. "No, love. We wait here. He'll be back. And if Andrew or Bill come looking for us, we need to be here."

Kelly's head dropped even as he drew in a deep breath. Worry covered his face and he felt fear in his heart. Lord? I can't do this. I can't lose my baby girl. Not like this. I know that You are in control. That nothing happens without You. And I know we are to trust and not fear. It's too hard, though, Lord.

He finally nodded, reaching to unlock the door and then shove it open.

"You're right, love. We will wait here. What can we do, though?"

"We spend time in prayer. We search for the verses that tell us not to fear but to trust. It's how we have always done it." Ruth's arm was around her husband, her heart heavy with worry.

"That we will." Kelly poured their coffee and then sat at the kitchen table beside Ruth, reaching for his Bible and then her hand. "We need to cover them in prayer, love. I have a bad feeling."

"So do I, Kelly." Ruth's voice cut off in a sob. She was used to dealing with crises but this was different. This was her daughter.

Andrew tapped at the back door and then opened it, walking in as the old family friend that he was. This time, though, he was here in his capacity as police chief. Bill followed him, his hand tucking away his phone as he did so.

Kelly was on his feet, approaching the men.

"Andrew? Bill?" He looked past them, a frown on his face. "You're here. Where is Saoirse? And Rowan? And Richard?"

Andrew shared a look with Bill before he reached to fill mugs of coffee for them both. Bill slid into a chair at the table, the folder that he carried laid down on the tabletop.

"We need to talk, Kelly. But first, as friends, can we pray with you?" Andrew sat, his eyes on first Kelly and then Ruth, watching as they shared a look.

"I guess." Kelly's eyes found Andrew's and saw the answer to his question in them. "I see, Andrew. Yes, let's pray. Then you two will tell us why you are here and just where Saoirse and Rowan are."

Chapter 23

Raising his head, Andrew studied the older couple. He had gotten to know them well over the past few years. Kelly was a staunch supporter of the police forces in the area, going well beyond what was needed to help fundraise and provide for the families.

"Kelly. Ruth. Richard was in an accident on the way here. Paul, one of his people, was driving and Silver, one of the ladies on his team, was with him. Paul has told us that he was boxed in and then run off the road. Their vehicle slammed into a tree. Richard, Paul and Silver were all injured. Richard is in surgery at the present time to repair damage to his shoulder. Silver is still unconscious. Paul is on his feet and very angry."

"Saoirse?" Ruth's voice was very quiet, almost too quiet for the men to hear.

"I'm sorry, Ruth. Kelly. Rowan and Saoirse were not in the vehicle. There is evidence that they were removed from the vehicle after the accident. We are investigating that even as we speak."

"But you have no idea where they are?" Kelly felt his hope drop as Bill shook his head.

"I'm sorry, Kelly. We don't. There is evidence of vehicles stopped on the side of the road but we don't see any evidence of where Rowan and Saoirse are and whether they were taken from the vehicle and put into another. We have called in our K-9 units to search but we will need to wait for daylight to do a foot search."

"I see." Kelly's eyes met Connell as he stopped just inside the door, shaking his head briefly at his son. "Where do we go from here?"

"We start searching. Unfortunately, we don't have any description of a vehicle or vehicles. Paul is not able to provide much of one other than they were trucks. He's fighting a

---

concussion among other injuries. We'll speak with him again tomorrow." Bill stared down at his folded hands. "We thought we had done the right thing, Kelly. Ruth. Richard is experienced in this. He didn't think that he needed all five of his team members."

"No, he shouldn't have had. But who knew he was heading this way? Ronan wouldn't have said anything." Kelly was puzzled.

"We're looking into that and speaking with the department in Oak City. We suspect that Ronan's place was being watched and when Richard left, he was followed." Andrew sat back, his thumb rubbing along the handle of his mug. "I'm sorry. I know I keep saying that. But I wish it had been different. We will do everything we can and more to find the two and bring them home."

"Thank you, Andrew. We know that you will." Kelly studied his hands. "What do you expect to happen from here?"

"That we don't know, Kelly. I'm being honest with you." Andrew shared a look with Bill. Both knew that the likelihood of the couple coming home was low. Whoever had taken them wanted something, and just what that something was, neither were sure. "I would like to set up a team here in case you get a ransom demand."

"Ransom? Really?" Ruth shook her head. "We're not rich, Andrew. We donate a lot of our income, keeping enough for expenses and future planning."

"I know, Ruth, but not many people would know that. Ransom can take many forms, other than just money."

"The artifacts?" Connell spoke from where he was leaning against the fridge. "Is that what they are after?"

"It's possible." Bill studied his friend. "Or it could be revenge of some kind."

"Revenge?" Kelly paled even further. "For what?"

"That's something one of our team has been researching. Lily has not said what she has found as of now." Bill looked down at his phone, which had been vibrating on the tabletop, touching it to bring up his messages. "I'm sorry. I need to run. Kelly, Ruth, Connell. You are in my prayers. I'll be back as soon as I can." Bill was gone before anyone could comment.

Andrew rose and followed him, stopping him near his vehicle.

"Bill?"

"Robert. He thinks he may have found something and wants me out there." Bill bit his lip as he stared into the distance. "A cigar butt. He says it's recent. How it didn't get run over or stepped on is amazing."

"God. God did that." Andrew rubbed at his face. "Connell will likely get the prayer chain working. I hate situations like this, Bill. We've had so many with our friends over the past couple of years."

"I know. With you and me and Silas as well." Bill turned. "I put in a call to Silas, asked that he and Madigan come over. Just said that they were needed. He was out of town but said he'd be here as soon as he could."

"Good. They're needed." Andrew nodded towards the street. "On your way, Bill. Keep me updated as to what is going on." Andrew looked around as he heard a car door closing and saw Phoebe approaching him, ready to walk into his arms. "Hello, sweetheart. You're here."

"I am, Drew. What is going on? I got the call from the prayer chain and felt God nudging me to come." She looked past him and paled. "Saoirse?"

"Yes. She and Rowan have disappeared." Andrew tightened his arms around his beloved wife, reliving in part their adventure. "I think we need to spend time with them, love, if you're up to it." He was concerned about Phoebe, knowing that their little one was due in about a month.

"I'm not that fragile, Andrew. I need to be here for them. I have my orders from God." She turned to face the house. "How are they?"

"In shock. Saoirse and Rowan were to come home today. Richard was bringing them. There was an accident and they disappeared."

"Oh, no!" Phoebe's face showed her shock. "Then, I guess we go in. I brought food, though I wasn't sure that I should."

"It's fine, sweetheart. In we go." Andrew walked her to the door, watching as she entered before he pulled out his phone. It was as he thought. No news, Bill had said. They were clearing out of the scene, leaving a patrol vehicle there over the night hours.

"How about Todd?" Connell stood beside him, having quietly returned, his face pale and taut, worry for his beloved sister on it.

"We'll see in the morning, Connell. Our K-9 units will search."

"But you don't think that they'll find anything. Bill said you were leaving the car there until morning."

"We are. Just for the dogs." Andrew prayed for his friend. "Phoebe brought some food, although she wasn't sure that she should have."

"It's fine. Mom will take it." Connell stared around his neighbourhood, seeing their neighbours watching. "We need to talk to the neighbours, tell them what's up."

"We'll do that, Connell. Our officers are starting a canvas here as they are around Ronan's and also Rowan's." Andrew pulled in a deep breath. "Connell, this is where it gets very hard. For all of you. The waiting. The fear. Make sure that you have someone to pray with and talk with."

Connell stared at him. "Andrew, will you be my partner in prayer?"

"I will, Connell. Now, in you go. We don't need you disappearing as well."

Chapter 24

The days dragged by, one after another. Ruth continued her time in her family practice while Kelly continued in his office. Neither was sleeping much, their time spent in prayer and conversation. Both feared for their daughter. Bill was around a couple of times a day, just checking in on them. He had shaken his head when they asked for news.

"I'm sorry, Kelly and Ruth. I have no news. We are working on it but for now, we are at a loss. We will not let this drop. That I can promise you." Bill had stayed for a while the day before, his eyes on the officer manning the set up in the office. There had been no ransom call.

Bill had finally walked away from his office the next day, heading for the downtown area. He searched for his contact there, a takeout cup of coffee and a muffin in a bag held in his hand. Sitting on the park bench near the centre of town, he waited, knowing that Sal would be around at some point. And he was correct. Sal slid down beside him, a hand out for the food.

Waiting until Sal had eaten the muffin, Bill finally spoke.

"What's the word, Sal?"

"The word? On who?" Sal was a source of information to Bill on many occasions but he liked to hide his words in sentences and questions that were not obvious to the casual listener.

Bill sighed. No, Sal was not making it easy for him, now was he, Lord?

"Saoirse. Rowan. What do you know about them?"

"Oh! Them! Yeah, I heard about them." Sal sipped at his cooling cup of coffee. "They're not in town."

"No? Any idea where?"

Sal shrugged. "Somewhere just outside the city is what I heard. On a farm somewhere."

"And do you know how many farms there are?"

Sal gave a quick grin. "I know. I've worked my share at times. I haven't heard which one. If I do, I'll find you." He dropped the empty cup into the garbage container as he rose. "One other thing, Bill. Scuttlebutt is that they're married."

Bill's head shot up as he stared after Sal as he walked away, his voice calling out to those he knew. *Married? They're not married. There is no way they'd do that, not without their parents and Connell present. Would they, Lord?* Bill shook his head as he rose and headed back for the office. He needed to do some research.

Pulling out his phone and glancing at the text message, Bill gave an exclamation and then ran for his vehicle. He sped towards Kelly's, seeing Kelly flying from his vehicle and into the house as he parked. Ruth was waiting for her husband on the front porch.

Bill stood watching the officer for a moment before he approached.

"Wayne? What do you have?"

Wayne, a younger officer, turned. "This. We were to open all the mail that was suspicious. This came today." He held out a photo for Bill to see. He had already sealed it into an evidence bag and marked it.

"What is it?" Bill studied his fellow officer before he took the photo. He could hear Ruth's faint sobs as Kelly cradled her to himself. He peered at the photo and drew in a breath. "Saoirse?"

"It is. She looks rough, Bill." Wayne stood, reaching for the phone log. "We also got a call. I haven't released it yet to her parents."

"Let's hear it." Bill reached for the headphones, a frown on his face that covered his shock and then concern. "Okay. We'll need to let them hear it."

—

"Bill?" Kelly had approached. "What is it? Is it worse than that photo?" His finger stabbed at the bag Wayne had laid back on the desk. His heart broke at the look on his daughter's face, the dazed look in her eyes, the bruising on her face, the lostness of her demeanour.

"It is. It's a ransom demand, Kelly." Bill reached to pull the plug on the headphones before he nodded at Wayne to replay the message.

"We have your daughter. We want what she had. We will be in touch. If you don't cooperate, you'll never see her again."

Kelly's face paled and he felt Ruth's hand on his back, her fingers clutching at his plaid flannel shirt.

"What do we have that they want? I don't understand." Ruth's voice held the sobs that she was trying hard to subdue.

"That's what we have to determine, Ruth. Other than the artifacts that we found, what else would she have?" Bill was puzzled as well. This was not going like any other kidnapping that he had ever dealt with.

"I don't get it, Bill. We never keep anything from where we go. We transport cargo across the province. On occasion, we head out to the mission fields with cargo and supplies that we are contracted to take. We don't take anything for that. Not one cent. It's part of our mission to honour God and be part of what we can do. We bring back no souvenirs. All our people know that and are adamant in refusing anything."

"We know, Kelly. We have talked to each one of your staff and pilots. They say the same thing." Bill rubbed a finger at his temple. The mild headache that he had awoken with had intensified. This was not helping. "The articles that we found in the plane? They are fake. Replicas."

"Could something be in them?" Ruth was puzzling through what Bill had said. "I mean, could someone have smuggled in jewels or something?"

Bill nodded. "We thought of that. We are going after a court order to destroy them." He didn't indicate to either of the older couples that word had come about smuggling going on from that country.

"But, what do we do about this?" Kelly gestured with his free hand towards the photo. "I want my daughter back, safe and sound."

"So do we, Kelly. So do we." Bill hesitated for a moment before he shook his head and excused himself. He needed to talk to someone and he just wasn't sure who.

Andrew looked up from his budget paperwork as Bill tapped at his door and he beckoned him into the room. Sitting back in his desk chair, the chair squeaking in protest, Andrew watched his friend, concern for him on his face.

"Bill?" Andrew finally spoke, a frown covering his face for a moment.

"Andrew? There was a ransom demand that had come through. And a photo showing Saoirse." Bill handed over the folder he had been opening and closing.

"That bad?"

Bill shook his head. "No. We've seen worse. We both have been through worse. It's the unknown that has me worried. I talked to Sal. He said that word on the street is that they are being held on a farm outside of town."

"A farm? That's interesting." Andrew sat forward, his hand resting on the closed folder. "Making them work, do you think?"

"It's possible. There are a number of farms that we know are just close to the edge of legitimacy. It would be a good cover." Bill rubbed at his temple.

"Take something for that headache and then come back." Andrew pointed to the door. "You've been fighting it all day, haven't you?"

"I have." Bill shoved himself to his feet and walked away, fatigue evident in his motions. Michael had been up and down all night and he had been the one getting up. Cora had been up as well but he had sent her back to bed, knowing that she would have to deal with the fractious youngster over the day.

Andrew watched him walk away before he opened the folder. A quickly indrawn breath showed his shock at the picture.

Bill is right. She looks rough. Lord, where are they? And how soon can we find them and rescue them? Rowan certainly doesn't need to be held captive again. Not after what he went through. We'll need to connect him with someone to talk with. I wonder if Doug's Darcie would be willing. He jotted down a note to call her.

Bill slid back into his seat, a mug of tea on Andrew's desk for him and a mug of coffee for himself set down on the table beside him.

"Andrew? Your thoughts?"

Andrew looked past Bill, his eyes focusing on the wall in front of him.

"She looks tired, Bill. And I can't tell if the bruises are from the accident or abuse."

"No, we can't. I would suspect abuse. If she was in the centre seat, she may not have hit anything."

"Just one of the others. And that could have left bruises. The phone call?"

"That. Kelly has no idea what she might have had. Ruth told me yesterday that she went through all of Saoirse's things, just looking for something that wasn't hers or seemed wrong. She found nothing. She just hopes that Saoirse will forgive her for doing that."

"I'm sure that she will. The court order?"

"Lily was walking over to get it today. She'll take it to the lab and then come find me if there is anything. What are your thoughts?"

"That I'm not sure of. I am not sure what would have been hidden in the articles. They really aren't that big. Jewels?"

"Maybe. Or a flash drive?"

"That's possible. But would they go to that extent?" Andrew sat back once more, his mug of tea in his hand as he sipped at it.

"Depends on who it is." Bill sat for a moment, not sure how to continue. "Sal mentioned something else."

Andrew's attention went back to Bill at the tone in his voice.

"And that would be?"

"He said scuttlebutt on the street is that Rowan and Saoirse are married. I can't see that."

Andrew hesitated. "No, I can't either, but we need to look into that." He turned to his computer. Pulling up a program, he searched before he drew a deep breath and looked over at Bill. "He's right, you know."

"He is? They are?"

"They are. There is a marriage registered to them. I don't recognize the minister, though." He searched further. "No wonder. He's not from our town. He's from a town three hours away. This is strange."

"Bizarre. How do we tell Kelly, Ruth and Connell? Or even Ronan and Lydia?"

"We keep this quiet for now, only telling them. I'll take that on, Bill. You go find Lily and see what she has discovered." Andrew watched Bill walk away again, a sigh drawn from him.

Lord, I have no idea what is going on. None of us do. But I do know that I have to trust You. That You are in control. That You have plans and purposes that we don't know about or even understand. This says our friends are married. Why and how? That is in Your hands and for us to discover.

Andrew took a look at his budget material and knew that he would have to work on it but first, he needed to find Kelly and Ruth. He glanced at the clock and then shook his head. *Later today,* he thought, *and he'd pay a visit with Phoebe in tow.*

Chapter 26

That evening, Kelly stepped back from their wooden front door to allow both Andrew and Phoebe to enter their wide entryway. Ruth had decorated it in soft colours with minimal furniture, wanting to leave it open and airy.

"Andrew? Phoebe? I wasn't expecting to see you tonight." Kelly pointed towards the kitchen. "Ruth is just finishing clearing the kitchen but we have tea ready. Do you have time?"

"We do, Kelly." Phoebe reached to hug him and held up a basket. "I have treats for you all, but I wasn't sure if they would be welcome."

"Your baking is always welcome. Go on through, Phoebe." Kelly watched Andrew, seeing the flicker of something in his eyes. "Andrew?"

"We need to talk, Kelly, but right at the moment, we are here as friends. How are you doing?"

Kelly shrugged. "I have no idea how to answer that question. Honestly? I am so numb that I don't know that I feel anything. Ruth is the same. Connell is vocal and I know that he has been spending time in the gym at work, taking out his frustration on the boxing bag. His chief has been around, concerned."

"Yes, I can see that. We will talk, Kelly. I have something that we need to discuss, but first, we pray with you both."

Andrew looked up as they finished their prayer time, watching his wife as she spoke with Ruth, drawing out how she was feeling. Phoebe has a knack for doing that, he thought. She has certainly been the helpmeet that I need as the police chief.

Kelly finally reached for Ruth's hand, his eyes on Andrew. He had heard Connell enter and then sit beside his father.

—

"Andrew? You said you needed to speak with us. What about?"

Andrew shared a look with Phoebe. He had not spoken with her about what he and Bill had discovered, but she was aware that something was troubling him. She had simply hugged him that evening when he arrived home and whispered a prayer in his ear and that she loved him.

"There is. And frankly, I have no idea how to say it."

"Just say it, Andrew." Ruth spoke. "I have found over the years that sometimes the blunt truth is the best. Is it about Saoirse?"

"It is and Rowan as well." Andrew's phone was out. "With your permission, I would like to call Ronan and Lydia."

"Actually, they are heading this way. In fact, that may be them now." Connell was on his feet, returning with Rowan's parents following him.

Andrew finally spoke, his eyes on the two mothers, feeling Phoebe's hand on his.

"Kelly, Ruth, Connell, Ronan, Lydia, what I am about to say must remain just with you for now. Bill and I have verified the facts. I have no idea how or when it happened but it did. Bill met with a contact this morning, who informed him that the scuttlebutt on the street is that Saoirse and Rowan are married." He waited patiently as the murmurs from the families filled the kitchen.

"Andrew? Is this true?" Ronan spoke. "But I don't understand."

"It is true, Ronan. I have verified it. How or why? That we don't know yet. I do know that it was a minister from a town a few hours away that performed the ceremony but it is registered in our town."

"I don't get it." Connell was on his feet, pacing the kitchen, running his hand through his hair. "She wouldn't do that."

"Not unless it meant saving Rowan's life." Ruth spoke with conviction.

"And the same for Rowan. He would marry Saoirse to save her." Lydia wiped at her face, the tears falling that she could not stop. "Anything else, Andrew?"

"There was a ransom call this morning. Not long enough to trace it. Bill and his team are working on it." Andrew looked around as he heard a knock at the door.

Connell returned, a strange look on his face.

"Andrew, there is a man at the door. He has asked for you specifically."

Andrew was on his feet, excusing himself and striding rapidly to the door, which he pulled closed behind him.

"Sal?"

"I know, Andrew. I'm not supposed to be here." Sal had changed his appearance from a down-and-outer to that of a businessman. "I had to. Word has come through where Rowan and Saoirse are being held. I had to come. Saoirse has been kind to me over the months that I have been on the streets."

"She has?" Andrew pointed to his car. "Inside there. I'll drive you to where you need to be for your appointment."

Sal nodded. "I do have that. At the detachment. I'm coming in, Andrew. I can't do this anymore."

"No, you've been past that point for days now, Sal." Andrew drove away before he parked in a shopping mall parking lot. "Okay. What have you got for me?"

"Here. This is where they are. I don't know how we missed it." Sal handed over a sheet of paper. "It's so close to town. A friend on the streets finally told me. They are running scared, Andrew, scared of whoever it is that is in charge. I don't know that we have that person yet."

"No, I don't think that we do." Andrew took the proffered paper and read through it. "That is close. Okay. So, you're coming

---

in. That's good. There's an opening on the detective squad if you want it."

"There is? I can take it?" Sal was surprised.

"You can. Come back in tomorrow and talk with Bill. He's in charge of the detectives now that William has retired. His slot is the one that we are filling. You'll do well on it." Andrew rubbed at his forehead with his thumb and forefinger. "I'm heading back to Kelly's. I'll call Bill and alert him."

"Already done. I spoke with him before I found you. He's setting up a team to go in tomorrow morning, real early he said."

"Good work. Now maybe we can finally get ahead of where we need to be."

Chapter 27

Standing in the shadows of the trees that surrounded the farmhouse early the next morning, Bill watched closely, looking for signs of anyone around. He frowned. It was too quiet, he thought. Granted, it was early, only just after four in the morning. He turned as he felt someone touch his arm.

"Anything, Bill?" Lily stood there, her face covered in a frown.

"No, it's quiet. Let's move in. I don't want to wait for too long just in case we're spotted." He glanced up at the sky. "It's starting to lighten somewhat. Everyone in place?"

"They are. We have the place surrounded. Patrol is covering the vehicles in the garage." Lily looked around. "We're set. Are you?"

"I am. Okay, let's move." Bill spoke quietly into his radio and watched as figures moved towards the house and the outbuildings. "We have no idea where they are."

"No. I would hazard a guess that they're in the house. Patrol will search the outbuildings."

Bill hammered at the front door, surprised not to rouse anyone before he reached for the doorknob. He frowned as it turned under his hand and the door opened. The officers entered, searching the building and then gathered outside.

"They were here, Bill." Lily spun in a circle. "But not now. Where?"

"Bring in the K-9's. See if they can find a trail." Bill was on the phone with Andrew. "Andrew? They're not here. They were, though. I'm bringing in the K-9's."

"Good move. I'm on my way. No sign at all?" Andrew's voice echoed over the phone.

"No, not today. But there is evidence that they were. In one of the bedrooms. There are two sets of leg shackles in the kitchen."

"Shackles? Unlocked or cut off?"

"Unlocked. I suspect that they were used if they were outside. The place is clean. I see Saoirse's work in that. Whether it was voluntary or not, that's the question."

"I would suspect that she was made to. And she would have objected and loudly." Andrew sighed, reaching for his mug of tea. He had been up all night and he was exhausted. He quietly slipped from his home, not seeing Phoebe standing at their bedroom window, her hand resting against it as she prayed for her husband and the others involved.

Andrew slowly walked towards Bill and Lily, his eyes on his detectives. *This is never easy, is it, Lord? Sometimes I wish I was still the lieutenant on the county force, but this is where You led me to. If I had not, I would not be where I can serve You best. Only today? This is not how I feel. I feel frustrated, empty, lost. I can't imagine how their parents and Connell are feeling.*

"Bill?" Andrew's quiet voice had the other man turning towards him.

"Andrew? You made good time." Bill nodded towards the house. "The techs are going through right now. But they were here. That much we know from the evidence." He looked towards the fields. "I wonder if they were made to work the fields."

"I would suspect so. This has been a market garden farm over the years. I can't say that it was ever on our radar for illegal activities."

"No, I don't think it was." Bill walked towards the fields, Andrew keeping pace with him. "This is not making sense, Andrew. I just don't get it."

"No, it's not. I would like to know where they are." Andrew turned as he heard his name called and waited for the tech to catch up with him. "Tracy?"

———

98

"I found this, Andrew." She held out an evidence bag. "It's a marriage certificate. It was tucked under a pillow in the bedroom that we think they were in."

He read it. "Rowan and Saoirse. We knew that they had been married. This is good. Keep it under your hat, Tracy. We don't want it getting out. Does anyone else know?"

She shook her head. "No. I was on my own. I need to get back there but I wanted to ask you about it."

"We had word yesterday that this had happened. Thanks, Tracy." Andrew watched as she ran back towards the house before he tucked the evidence bag into an inside jacket pocket. "I don't understand, just like you, Bill."

"No, it's strange. Were they forced to marry?"

"I would suspect that was the case. But as to why? That we won't know until we find them. And find them we must."

The two men looked up as they heard their names called and then ran towards the officer heading their way.

"Stan? What do you have?" Bill slid to a halt beside him as the officer paused to catch his breath.

"We have tracks. Cole says Keene has picked up a scent and is following it. It's fresh from what he said."

"Where?" Bill and Andrew followed him.

"Cole?" Bill's voice caught the K-9 officer's attention and he spun.

"There. Keene has a trail. I stopped him to allow you to catch up." He watched his dog closely. "He's eager to get moving."

"Then let's go." Bill pointed towards the dog. "Where's he heading?"

"Towards the cliffs." Cole paused. "I hope that's not where they are."

"We'll know soon enough."

Chapter 28

Andrew's fear for the younger couple grew the closer they came to the cliffs. He watched Bill's face as the dawn lightened the sky and saw the same look in his eyes. *It is different, isn't it, Lord,* Andrew mused, *when it's someone that we know? I pray for their safety.*

Bill cautiously approached the edge of the cliff and with his hand tight in Cole's, leaned over.

"We'll need better lighting. I can't see if there's anything there."

Cole nodded as he pulled Bill back from the edge. "I know. Stacy's gone after lighting. Keene says that they're here." Keene had sat in his normal position for finding someone. "He's not acting as if they're dead. He has a different demeanour if they are."

"That's good. I know you trust him." Andrew looked around. "Okay. Seal off this area. Only the necessary personnel here. Bill?"

Bill was distracted from what Andrew was saying, his eyes catching something. A flash of something in the light. He moved down the edge of the cliff, following it before he gave a shout.

"I see them, Andrew. Down on that slope. We'll need rescue." Bill moved back carefully from the edge. "They're down there, but I don't see any movement."

Cole watched Keene. "He knew, Bill. He knew they were there." He tossed the tug that he held in his hands to the dog, who brought it to him to play with. He tugged for a few minutes before he released the dog.

Andrew watched as the firemen approached, a groan coming from him. Bill turned to him in surprise.

"Connell."

———

"Connell? He's here?" Bill sighed as well. "He'll want to go down. And there's not much we can do to prevent it."

"No. Let's head over and talk to the captain."

Connell looked around as he heard voices and his face paled as he recognized Bill and Andrew.

"Bill? Andrew?" He spun to stare at the cliffs before a cry was wrung from him. "No! Not that!"

"They're there, Connell." His captain's hand rested on his shoulder. "I'll send someone else but you're the best we have in these rescues."

"I'll go." They watched as Connell straightened up, his spine going stiff. "I have to, Cap. I have to. That's my little sister down there."

"Okay, then. Off you go. Jay, you're with him?"

"I am, Cap."

Cap turned to Andrew and Bill. "He'll be a professional, even though his heart is hurting. He's one of the best I have."

"We know, Cap." Andrew and Bill followed Cap as he walked towards the men setting up on the edge of the cliff. "Paramedics are here?"

"They're on their way. I asked for the best of them as well." Cap sighed. "Saoirse is family, you know. Being Connell's sister, she's family to the men and ladies of our crews. They have been hurting for him. All of them have been out looking on their own time. Even when they are at work, they're searching."

"As have our people." Bill agreed. He stopped, his eyes on Connell. "This is going hard on him."

"As it should." Andrew's heart raised in prayer. *Lord, I have no idea what they'll find. But I do know that You are in control. In the chain of life, as we call it, You number our days and our walk. You know what we will each face and have already gone before us. You promise that in Your work. Please, dear Lord? Don't let Saoirse be deceased. That would be devastating for this young man, my friend who cares so deeply.*

Bill had turned to speak with Andrew, stopping as he saw the look on his face, and nodded. *He's praying him through this, isn't he, Lord? Andrew does that. He prays us through whatever it is that we face. And his Phoebe is doing the same. I wonder if she has found Cora yet. Those two are our prayer warriors, Lord.*

Cora turned from the window, her eyes on Phoebe who was pouring out tea for them both. Michael had found Phoebe's kitten and was minding his mother's admonition not to pull the kitten's tail. He had nodded and agreed not to, instead feeding the kitten its kibble piece by piece. Cora smiled. Bill and she had talked about getting a kitten for Michael and she decided that they would, soon. He needed that.

"Cora? Here. Sit." Phoebe sank into her chair, her hand rubbing at her abdomen. "This little one is active today. I don't know how you did it."

"With grace and God, that's how we do it, Phoebe. Have you spoken with Andrew this morning?"

Phoebe shook her head. "It was quite early when he left. In fact, he had never been to bed at all. I watched him leave. I am afraid, Cora. Afraid for our friends."

"I am too. I haven't spoken with Bill. I don't even want to text him. He said that they were heading out early this morning to search somewhere. He didn't give a lot of detail."

"They never do." Phoebe watched as Michael cuddled her little calico kitten. "They can't but they know that we will pray for them."

"And we shall. Then I feel that we need to find the families and be with them."

"I agree. I spoke with Madigan earlier. She was awake around four and bathed our men and those families in prayer. She said that she and Silas would head that way. He had a meeting earlier this morning but when he was done he would come for her." Phoebe shook her head. "I never in my life imagined that we would be friends like this. And all mothers around the same time."

Cora grinned. "I know. Madigan was always adamant that she never wanted to be a mother. That she was not mother material. She is. She just didn't want to hope, I think. She never expected to marry."

"And to marry in that way? Oh, my! Who would have thought?" Phoebe's hand reached for Cora's. "Let's pray, Cora. Andrew calls us his prayer warriors. We need to do that. We are in a war for Saoirse and Rowan."

Chapter 29

His heart in his mouth, Connell nodded at the men holding his rope, his gloved hands tight on it. *Lord, this is it, isn't it? Do I find my sister alive or dead? He nodded at Jay and they began their descent, landing lightly on the outcropping of rock, that was cliff-like in appearance. He stared for a moment, taking in the area. He saw the rock at the end of the cliff and wondered. Lord, did You do that? Place that rock to prevent them from going any further. And just how did they get there?*

He knelt beside Rowan, Jay on the other side, a frown on his face. Rowan's right arm was tight around a small tree, his other arm holding Saoirse tight to his side. Both seemed to be unconscious. His hand shaking, Connell reached for Saoirse, his head dropping in relief as he found a pulse.

"Jay?"

"He's alive, Connell. And awake." Jay studied the other man. "Rowan, is it? Are you hurt?"

"I don't know." Rowan's eyes blinked. "Where am I?"

"On a cliff. And holding onto a tree with all your might." Connell's voice had Rowan turning that way. "And you're holding on to my sister."

"I am?" Rowan's eyes dropped. "I am. I was so afraid." His breath came in gasps, evidence of the pain that he was in. "We were running in the dark and then the ground just disappeared. We rolled and I grabbed tight to her. I slid down and something stopped me. It hurt my legs when it did. I laid for a bit until I could catch my breath. I reached for that tree and tried to pull us up and back to the cliff but I just couldn't. Is Saoirse okay?" He was becoming agitated.

"Relax, Rowan. She's unconscious. Let's get you two up and then to help."

104

With the assistance of the paramedics who had been lowered down to them, the two men worked quickly to assess the couple and then reached for the wire-frame basket stretchers that had been lowered. They moved the couple to backboards, neck collars in place, before transferring them to the stretchers. Connell stood for a moment, his eyes on the edge of the outcropping, thanks to the Lord rising in his heart. He didn't know how badly hurt his sister was but she was safe with them once more. She would be coming home.

He rappelled back up the cliff, hands reaching to pull him up and over and steady him before he was shrugging out of his equipment and then heading towards the stretchers. Connell needed to know how Saoirse was.

"Peter?"

Peter, a good friend and one of the best paramedics on the force, turned.

"She's alive, Connell. Right now, I can't tell you how hurt she is. Only the physicians can do that." He nodded towards Cap. "Right now, Cap's waiting for you. Head off. We're going that way shortly."

"I'll help carry the stretcher." Connell stood staring down at her before he looked towards Rowan.

Rowan was awake and in pain, that much was evident. Jay approached Connell.

"He's fighting them, Connell. He thinks Saoirse is lost."

"From their history, I can only imagine how he feels." Connell moved to crouch down beside Rowan. "Rowan?" He had to speak twice before Rowan looked at him. "She's here. They're looking after her."

"Where? I can't find her."

Connell's hand on his chest kept him still. "She's beside you, Rowan. We're heading off with you two." He paused, a question on his face. "I have one question. Is it true?"

Rowan's movements stopped as he stared up at Connell.

"I don't understand. Is what true?"

"Are you two married?" He kept his voice low enough so that only Rowan could hear him. "Andrew said you were."

Rowan's eyes slid shut and pain crossed it, pain not from his injuries.

"I had to, Connell. I had to. They would have made her marry one of their men. I couldn't let that happen. I had to save her." He drifted off to unconsciousness at that, not realizing that Andrew and Bill had heard his words as well.

Bill frowned, that thought never having crossed his mind. He reached for Rowan's stretcher, his hand grasping it firmly as he helped to carry him back across the rough ground to the waiting paramedic rigs. He stood back, the frown still on his face before he turned. Andrew stood beside him, his face blank.

"Did you think that, Andrew?" Bill's voice was low.

"I did, Bill. It was something that Kelly had asked me when we were talking last night. We were walking in their backyard and he was trying to understand. He wanted to know if Rowan would have done that to save her from something. I guess that we have our answer."

"Somewhat. I still don't get it."

"Doesn't matter if we do or don't. The deed is done and they're married. Now, we just have to fill in all the blanks, answer all the questions, and then help them to heal."

"It's going to be hard on Rowan. The second time as a captive. This time it was only what three weeks or so?"

"About that, but it would seem like a lifetime to him." Andrew turned, watching the activity happening around them. "I'm heading off, Bill. Catch up with me later."

Bill nodded, his attention going back to where Tracy was waiting. He walked towards her, his head tilting as he noticed her agitation.

"Tracy?"

"Bill? Who was with them?" She stumbled over her words. "Who was with them?"

"Tracy, you're repeating yourself. What do you mean? Who was with them?"

Tracy thrust another evidence bag at him. "This. Who was with them? Someone was on our side, I can tell you that." She pointed. "That's not one of their captors. They would not have left that for us to find."

Bill studied the note. "No, you're right. It's not one of them. I have no idea who it is. Work what you can with your magic on it. And come find me at some point today. We'll be here for a while and then I'm heading back to the office."

Tracy stared at the cliff and then towards where she could hear the rigs leaving.

"How are they, Bill?"

"They're alive. Rowan took the brunt of it, I gather. We'll know more later." He turned her back towards the farm. "What else do you need to tell me?"

Chapter 30

Turning back to face the front door as Kelly answered it, Andrew reached to shake his friend's hand.

"I'm glad you're here, Kelly. Is Ruth?"

"She is. Ronan and Lydia are here as well. So are Cora, Phoebe, Madigan, and Silas. Know anything about that?" Kelly's sense of humour briefly surfaced.

"No, but I thought my wife would be as would Bill's. It doesn't surprise me that our minister and his wife are here. Where is everyone?"

"In the sunroom. We are just having a bite to eat. Join us?" Kelly led the way.

"I would like that. But we need to talk, Kelly, and now."

Kelly spun to stare at Andrew, seeing the answer in his eyes. Kelly's own eyes slid closed and tears trickled down his face, startling Ruth as she approached.

Ruth's face paled and she began to shake her head.

"Not that, please, Lord." Her voice caught the attention of the others in the room who rose, Ronan and Lydia approaching.

"We have them. They are on their way to the hospital right now." Andrew watched with compassion as the four older adults struggled to comprehend his words.

Hope flowed through the four.

"You have them?" Ronan spoke, his voice so much like his son's, his wife wrapped in his arms.

"We do. We found them about an hour ago. Connell was there. I'm not sure if he's back at work or if Cap has released him to follow his sister. We'll head out but first, we pray." He looked up at Silas. "Silas? We could use some of your prayers."

"With pleasure. Dear Lord, we bring You all our thanks that we have both Saoirse and Rowan back with us. Your hand was on them. We don't need to know the details right now, dear Lord. It is sufficient that they are alive and with us. Guide the medical staff as they treat. Be with each one of their parents and with Connell. Thank you, gracious and merciful Father. Amen." Silas looked around. "How we be head in? We'll take Ronan and Lydia. Andrew?"

"I guess that leaves me with the other three. Phoebe?" He watched for a moment.

"Cora and I will tidy up here, Ruth, if you will leave a set of keys for us. We'll meet you there." Phoebe reached for the keys that Kelly extended towards her. "Go. We'll be there shortly."

Cora watched from the doorway as they left.

"I am so thankful, Phoebe. I didn't think that they would be alive when we found them." She turned back to find her friend fighting tears and simply moved to hug her. "Emotions. All over the place. We have a good reason though today."

Phoebe nodded, reaching to wipe at her cheeks with her hands before she stared at them.

"We do, Cora, but it's not over. Not by a long shot as Drew's father would say. There are still people out there that want something or someone." Horror coursed through her, causing Cora to reach out and grasp her hands. "I had a horrible thought. What if it is revenge and directed towards Kelly through Saoirse?"

"That makes sick sense, you know." Cora moved away, gathering up the food that had not yet been touched in the sunroom and heading for the kitchen with it. Phoebe followed with the tray of dishes. "Here. I'll grab the beverages and the cream and sugar and mugs. You put the food away."

Ronan, Lydia, Kelly, and Ruth almost ran into the hospital, searching for someone who could answer their questions. Connell approached his parents, still in uniform. Cap had sent him to the hospital, finding someone to cover the rest of his shift. He knew how close the siblings were.

"Connell?" Ruth hugged her son and then stood, her hands on his arms. "Any word?"

"Not yet, Mom. She was unconscious when we found them." Connell bit at his lip. He had been warned by Bill not to tell his parents or Rowan's how or where they had been found. That had to come from the officials. "Rowan was at first, but he did rouse."

"He did?" Lydia reached to hug Connell, holding on just a little bit longer, missing hugging her own son. "He's okay?"

"I don't know yet, Lydia. I'm sorry. The physicians are with them." He bit at his lip again, a habit his father recognized.

Kelly looked around, finding an area that was clear and where they could talk.

"Over here. We'll wait here." He waited until they were all seated before he laid a hand on his son's shoulder. "Something is bothering you, son. Talk to me."

Connell nodded, his eyes on his boots, seeing the dust and dirt that had gathered on them over the day.

"I asked Rowan."

"I don't understand. You asked him what?" Kelly's eyes found the other three and then raised to see their friends gathered around them, providing a wall to curious eyes. Bill stood waiting, he could tell, to speak with them.

"I asked if it was true. That they were married." Connell looked up, an unreadable look in his eyes. "He said that it was true. That he had to."

"He had to?" Ronan spoke up. "I don't understand either, Connell. What did he mean?"

Connell stared at them, devastation on his face, devastation for his sister and Rowan.

"He said that he had to. He didn't have a choice. They were going to make her marry one of their men. He couldn't let that happen."

There were indrawn breaths from the families before Bill spoke.

"What else did he say, Connell?"

Connell looked up at Bill, shaking his head. "That was it. That he had to do that. That he couldn't let it happen. What did he mean, Bill?" Connell hurt for his little sister. They were close, these two, and he didn't want her hurt, not any more than she had been.

Chapter 31

An hour passed and then another. Both Kelly and Ronan paced the waiting room of the Emergency Department and then moved outside, not speaking but silent in companionship. Connell paced with them, his mind not on them but instead on what Rowan had said. He had puzzled it out over and over and still had not quite decided what he had meant.

Lydia found Ronan at last and pulled him back inside.

"We can see him, Ronan. But Rowan is adamant that he needs to get up and find Saoirse. He's afraid that she has disappeared."

Ronan nodded. "I see. Then, let's find our son, shall we?"

Hearing a commotion from his room, they hurried in, stopping short as they did so, the door swinging closed behind them. Rowan was on his feet, pulling out the IV line much to the distress of the nurse. He was shaking his head, his words loud in the room.

"I need to find Saoirse. I need to find my wife. Where is she?" He turned as he heard the footsteps. "Dad? Mom? Can you help me? They won't tell me where Saoirse is? Is she here?"

"She is, son, but you need to be back in that bed." Ronan's hand on his arm stopped him for a moment.

Rowan shook off his father's hand.

"Where is she, Dad? Can you help me find her?"

The plaintive plea in his son's voice broke Ronan's heart. He remembered hearing that tone when his son was a toddler and couldn't find something that he wanted or needed.

"I will, son. Here. Let's go out into the hallway but you have to be quieter." Ronan linked an arm with Rowan, seeing Lydia doing the same. "We'll find her for you. Nurse?"

"She's next door, but he can't see her. He's not kin to her." The nurse was angry with Rowan.

"But you see, he is. They are married. So you really can't keep them apart, now can you?" Lydia turned a stern look towards the nurse, who flounced by her, intent on keeping the young couple apart.

Rowan stood for a moment, catching his breath and his balance before he turned.

"Which room, Dad?"

Connell appeared at that point. "Rowan? You're on your feet. You shouldn't be."

"I know. But I need to find Saoirse. Where is she?"

"Right here. Mom sent me to find out if you were on your feet. She seemed to think that you would be." A brief hint of humour flickered across his face. "Ronan? Lydia? What was he up to?"

"He was on his feet and arguing with the nurse. By the way, who is she? She was adamant that Rowan could not see Saoirse." Lydia looked around for her. "Her attitude needs a lot of work."

"It does. She's always been like that. The physician will talk with her. Right in here, Rowan. I'll wait out here for you." He watched as Rowan hesitated for a moment before he shoved open the door. He frowned as he saw the dirt and the tears on Rowan's clothes.

"We'll need to get him some clean clothes." Lydia looked around. "Who can we send?"

"Silas will go. He and Madigan have offered to do that."

"Oh, thank you." Ronan turned. "I'll go find him."

Connell's hand stopped him. "He's already gone, Ronan. He volunteered to do that. Madigan is with him. They'll bring in clean clothes for them."

———

113

Lydia reached to hug him once more. "You have a wonderful church family, Connell. Many of them have reached out to us over the past few weeks, making sure that we didn't want or need anything. It is a blessing to have that."

"They are a great family, I must say. They go over and above what they need to." Connell slumped against the wall, his body shaking slightly with fatigue but also his emotions. "What can I do for you?"

"For us? Take care of yourself." Ronan's hand rested on Connell's shoulder. "I know that you have been searching, not sleeping, working in a dangerous job. We are fine. But you, young man? You need to take care."

Chapter 32

Kelly and Ruth had looked up as they heard their names called and were on their feet, heading for the physician.

"Theodore? You're working today." Kelly reached to shake the physician's hand, a friend from church and also a member of their deacon board.

"I am. I'm glad. Let me take you to Saoirse. I don't know what she has been through but she is one fortunate lady. The Lord was looking after her."

"That He was. Her injuries?" Ruth hesitated before she asked. "That is if you can tell us. We're not her first next of kin anymore."

"No, I understand that. But Rowan is not in a position right at the moment to disagree with me talking to you. I'm sure it's okay." He paused. "She has bumps, bruises, a concussion. I don't know what she's been going but her hands are nicked and cut. They are covered with healing blisters."

"They are? Oh! They said that they thought she and Rowan were on a farm." Kelly shared a look with Ruth.

Theodore shot them a quick look before he responded.

"I see. So this is all new to you as well." He shoved open a door. "In here. I'll be back in a bit. Connell, in you go as well. We'll let all of you in. When Rowan's on his feet, he'll be in here as well."

Connell snorted. "That will be soon, I would suspect, Theodore."

Ruth covered her mouth with her hand, tears on her face, as her other hand reached for her daughter. She gently touched Saoirse's face.

Kelly drew in his breath sharply as he studied his daughter. He felt the anger growing in him towards whoever it was. He knew that was wrong but it still happened. He would deal with it later, he decided. He knew Connell was on the other side of the bed and raised his eyes to find Connell's face shuttered. Connell had had time to adjust his thinking and to some degree his emotions before he saw Saoirse again.

Theodore paused as he entered the room, a hand holding open the door before he approached them.

"She's had a rough go, Kelly and Ruth. You can see that by her looks. What her mental status is at present, we don't know. Just a question. When did Rowan and she marry?"

"Sometime over the last few weeks. We don't know. We weren't told." Kelly didn't see the look on Theodore's face. "Any broken bones or anything like that?"

"No, no broken bones. Even in her fall, she didn't break anything."

"Fall?" Ruth looked around. "What fall?"

Theodore looked at the parents. "You weren't told? Then I'll have to have Bill speak with you. He's the one to tell you how she was found." He shared a look with Connell, who nodded.

Connell drew in a deep breath. He could tell his parents the circumstances as to how the couple was found, but that was not his place. His place was just to be a big brother. To pray for her and then try and protect her as best he could. He sighed again. Only this time? He had to step aside for Rowan, and he wasn't quite sure how he liked that idea.

Finally stepping away and outside, Connell rubbed at his face and then stood leaning against the wall. He nodded at the nurses and physicians and other healthcare workers as they passed him. He knew most of them. One man caught his eye. He was out of place, Connell decided, not sure why he thought that. He saw Bill approaching him.

"Connell? How are they?"

"Saoirse still out of it. Rowan? I have no idea." He looked around. "That man there? The one dressed as a janitor? He doesn't seem to fit. I've never seen him before and I know most of those who work this department."

"Is that right?" Bill looked around as well and then headed away, following the man. He stopped him and then a hand to his arm led him away. He sighed to himself. Who next would be the one he would have to arrest?

Looking up at last as he heard the door in front of him opening, Connell shoved away from the wall and approached Rowan. He could see the agitation in Rowan and looked past him at Ronan and Lydia. He nodded to himself. He's in love, I can see. He had better be. Then he asked for forgiveness. It was not his place to decide if Rowan should love his sister or not. That was between them.

"Rowan?"

"Where's Saoirse? I need to find her." Rowan's agitation was growing moment by moment.

Taking pity on him, Connell directed him to the room next door, watching as Rowan stumbled as he walked through the door, his fatigue and pain evident. He turned to Lydia and Ronan.

"You two okay?"

Ronan shrugged. "Our emotions are all over the place, I guess you could say. How about your parents?"

"The same, I suspect." Connell turned at that point, heading for the waiting room, Ronan and Lydia keeping pace with him. "They'll want to know how they are. I have no idea what to say."

"Just say that Rowan is on his feet. Saoirse is not. They'll understand." Lydia reached to hug Connell again. "Just keep trusting, Connell, no matter how hard it is."

———

Chapter 33

Letting the door swing closed behind him, Rowan stiffened his spine and his knees as he wobbled for a moment. He was weak, he knew, and not just from the fall or whatever it was that had happened late the night before. He had been working on little food and little sleep, staying awake as much as he could to watch out for Saoirse. He had slept, when he did, with his body against the door just so he could stop whoever it was that would enter.

He approached the bed, sensing there were others in the room but his focus was solely on Saoirse. He stopped short of the bed, his eyes on her as she lay still on her side facing away from the door. Walking around the bed, Rowan reached to touch her face, his hand cupping her cheek as his thumb rubbed against it. He felt her nestle into his hand and sighed.

Lord, what have I done? I married her to save her but I'm no longer sure that was the right thing to do. We didn't have much time to decide. Not and keep her safe. That Evan, whoever he is, made sure that we were okay before he left with the minister and the minister's wife. I have no idea who they were but they certainly didn't want to be there, that much I know. They didn't seem to have much choice.

Saoirse roused somewhat at feeling Rowan's welcome touch. She had been so afraid when they had been taken. She was afraid for Rowan, knowing that he was putting himself in harm's way to protect her. He had done that just a few days earlier when he had stepped in and married her. That had not gone well.

Her eyes opened but everything seemed blurry. She blinked, not able to clear the haze.

"Rowan?"

"Right here, sweetheart. We're safe." Rowan bent over the bed, his hand clutching at the bed rail to steady himself.

"We are? Where are they?"

"They're not here. Just us. We're safe, sweetheart."

"We are? Rowan, you're blurry."

Rowan gave a half-smile. "I am? I think you have a concussion, sweetheart. Running through the fields in the dark? You fell a couple of times."

"I did, didn't I? And I took you down with me at least once. Where are they, Rowan? Will they come and make us work today?"

"No, not today, sweetness. They're not here." Rowan's eyes raised and he saw for the first time Kelly and Ruth standing on the other side of the bed, puzzled looks on their faces. "Your Mom and Dad are here."

"They are? Oh, no! They're captives too."

"No, we're free, sweetness." He bent to drop a kiss on her cheek. "We'll be able to leave soon."

"We can?" Saoirse closed her eyes, a deep sigh rising from within her. "Take me home, please, Rowan."

"I will. I'll take you to your parents'."

"No, your home."

"I don't have one, remember? I gave up my apartment to move here."

"You did? Why did you want to move here?"

"Because there is a beautiful lady who lives in this town who happens to be my wife."

"There is?" Saoirse's eyes flickered open. "We'll find you a house. We'll make it a home. Take me home, please, Rowan?"

"I will, sweetness. As soon as the doctor says you can leave, we'll leave." Rowan waited for Saoirse to speak again. When she didn't, he simply stood and watched her.

"Rowan?" Kelly's voice finally broke through the silence. "What happened?"

———

119

Rowan shook his head. "I have to talk to Bill or someone first. I have a statement to give." He watched closely as Kelly and Ruth shared a look. "We'll talk, Kelly. I'm sorry that Saoirse and I did what we did, marry without our families there."

"But you had to, didn't you? To protect her?" Ruth walked around the bed to hug Rowan. "In that case, there is nothing to forgive. You put your own life on the line, I suspect, to do that."

Rowan nodded, a sober look on his face. "I did, Ruth. More than once." He bit at his lip and then turned back to watch Saoirse. "When can she leave?"

"Soon, Rowan." Kelly turned as the door opened and Theodore entered. "Here's Theodore. He can let us know more."

"More what?" Theodore studied his friends and then turned to Rowan. "And you would be Rowan?"

"I am." Rowan straightened up taller. "When can Saoirse go home? She's been awake but says her vision is blurry."

"She has been, has she? The blurry vision? That's concerning but it could be the concussion. Just what did you two go and do?"

"Went over a cliff, if I remember rightly." Rowan didn't hear the soft sounds from Kelly and Ruth. "My legs hurt from hitting whatever it was that stopped us."

"And I would hazard a guess that you took the brunt of the fall to protect Saoirse?" Theodore's kindly eyes assessed the younger man. "You don't have to say it out loud, Rowan. I can see the answer on your face. Now, as to Saoirse?" He looked up at Rowan as he finished his assessment. "You're taking her to Kelly and Ruth's?"

"I have to. I don't have a home here, not yet anyway." Rowan's eyes were on Saoirse, his heart in them for the others to see. "You see, I gave up my apartment to move here before we were kidnapped. I don't have a home to take her to."

"You have a home with us, Rowan. And with your parents." Kelly's arm rested on Rowan's shoulders just as he would have done to his own son. "You're family, Rowan. Make no mistake about that."

"I am, I guess. Not how we would have wanted it." Rowan raised his head, a sheepish look on his face. "I didn't leave Mom and Dad very well."

"They understand, Rowan. They're waiting with Connell." Ruth linked an arm with him. "We'll go find them and then I'll come back. She can go soon, Theodore?"

"I think so. We've done the imaging and the blood work that we need to. Everything is fine that way. But she does seem to have a concussion. Watch her closely, Ruth, as I know you will. I don't have to tell you what to watch for."

"No, you don't. This is one time that I dislike being a family physician. I know too much."

Theodore grinned at her disgruntled words. "That you do, but it's for the best. God knew that you would be in this position, don't you know that? That's why you're here."

"He did, didn't He?" Ruth agreed as she moved away, drawing both Kelly and Rowan with her.

Chapter 34

Carrying Saoirse into the house, Rowan hesitated, not sure where to head with her. Ruth took pity on him and pointed towards the sunroom.

"In there, for now, I think, Rowan. It's her favourite room. It might help when she awakes to see it." Ruth hurried away to find a pillow and blanket for her daughter, to stand and watch the gentleness with which Rowan was treating Saoirse.

Rowan laid his bride down on the sofa and reached for the pillow to tuck it gently under her head and then stood back as Ruth covered her daughter. He was on his knees beside the sofa when Ruth finished, an arm around Saoirse as his head bowed in prayer.

Ruth stood back, fighting her tears before she turned and almost ran from the room, finding Kelly waiting just outside the door, his arms open to cradle Ruth to him. He felt her body shaking with her sobs and felt his own tears on his face. He could hear Connell in the kitchen, moving as quietly as he could.

Connell looked around as he heard the door close and Bill appeared. He held up the coffee pot as Bill nodded, his briefcase hitting the floor near the door.

"Where are they?" Bill took the mug with a quiet thank you.

"In the sunroom. Saoirse is still out of it. I don't know that you'll get much out of her today."

"Not likely. That's okay. I'll be around. We'll keep the officer and the equipment here for a while. Richard was asking about them, whether we had found them."

"He was? How is he?" Connell was pulling out the loaf of bread and then meat and sandwich fixings. He glanced at the clock. Close enough, he thought, to a mealtime to eat.

"Healing and still angry. He's working through that. This is the first time, he said, that anyone has been hurt this bad. His team is hurting as well."

"I'm sure that they are. He'll be around at some point, won't he?" Kelly took up the conversation.

"He will. Now, I need to speak with Rowan. May I go on through?"

"You can, Bill. You don't need to ask." Ruth reached for her cup of tea, her eyes on Bill.

"As a friend, no, I don't. This is official, Ruth. I need to ensure that all the steps are covered. That means asking for permission to go anywhere here in your home or on your property." He searched the faces of the ones gathered, who now included Ronan and Lydia. "I'll talk with him and then let you all rest and relax for a day or so."

Bill stood for a moment, watching Rowan before he moved forward, to set their mugs of coffee on the low table near Rowan. He reached to draw Rowan to his feet and to a chair, seeing the fatigue weighing Rowan down.

"Rowan?" Bill's voice held a touch of amusement.

"Bill? You're here." Rowan rubbed at his face. "Yeah, I guess you would be. You want to talk."

"We need to. But first, here's a mug of coffee for you. Connell was making sandwiches. I'll go get you one."

"Bill? Thanks. And can you find some juice for Saoirse, please? She needs that."

"I will." Bill was as good as his word, back with their food and the juice that Rowan had requested. "She's still sleeping?"

"She is. Theodore said that she would but that we needed to awaken her every few hours." Rowan's eyes were on her. "I don't know that I have the heart to do that."

"It's necessary, Rowan, given her concussion. Ruth will help."

———

123

"I know that she will." Rowan finished his sandwich and then sat, his hands cradling his mug. "Do you know how much I longed to be able to get her away? There was just no opportunity. Not until last night. We had help. I fear for Evan's life though."

"Evan? Who's he?"

Rowan frowned. "He was one of our captors, but he didn't seem to fit. He was kind to us, gentle with Saoirse. He stood guard during the day as we worked the fields. He disappeared at night. I never knew where he went but he was always back in the early morning hours."

"I see." Bill sipped at his coffee, content to wait for Rowan to be ready to start. "I'll take your statement when you're ready, Rowan. I'll get Saoirse's tomorrow. I won't rouse her now, not unless she awakens and can give it."

Rowan nodded, his eyes on Saoirse as she slept. His mind wandered back in time, back to when he had found out that she was in danger. He had acted impulsively, he knew, but he would not take back his actions even if he could. He had felt driven to try and find her and protect her. That was true even now. He had tried his best during this second captivity of his to do just that. He had succeeded for the most part. And he had had some help, he had to acknowledge. Lord, *You provided Evan to be there. You protected us as we worked and lived in that house. I have no idea what could have happened if You had not.*

He finally looked at Bill and spoke.

"I'm ready, Bill. It's not pretty."

"It never is, Rowan. Just for the record? Both Cora and I were kidnapped after we married. We almost didn't make it. My first wife was killed by an experimental drug that Cora's first husband was involved in manufacturing and testing. She didn't know that. He was killed on their wedding day. We connected again when she returned here to our hometown. So I can understand to a certain extent what you are saying. Now, let's get your statement and then I'll leave."

Chapter 35

Rowan nodded, his eyes on Bill's face, shock briefly showing in his eyes at Bill's words. You would never know, he thought, as he pictured the couple and their happiness.

"I didn't know, Bill."

"No reason that you would have. Andrew and Phoebe? He married her the day after he pulled her from a roadhouse. He had been asked to save her. And Silas and Madigan? She found a body in the flooded basement of the church and that led to their adventure. And yes, they married as well to save one another. So you see, you're in good company." Bill's attention went to his laptop, not seeing the surprise and then understanding on Rowan's face. "Okay, Rowan, we're all set. Just give your statement as you can. We'll go over it. I'll clarify what I need to. Then I'll print it off and you can sign it." Bill was on his feet, out of the room and then back with water bottles. "Here. Just in case you need it. I suspect this will take a while."

"It will." He reached for the bottle. "Thanks, Bill, for all you have done. I know that you have worked many hours on this while working other cases."

"I have and so have many others." Bill looked up from where he had been booting up his laptop. "Whenever you are ready, Rowan. I'll just note the date and time and who is present." He slid a glance towards Saoirse, noting that she was still asleep.

Rowan nodded, his eyes on Saoirse as well, not quite sure how to begin.

"Okay, I guess I'll start." His voice died away, Bill's eyes on him as he spoke, faint amusement lurking in them. "I just don't know where to."

"The beginning is usually the right place. We have your statement as to what happened in the other country. That plays a part, we know, in what happened here. We'll discuss that later. But for now? Start where you were travelling back here."

Rowan nodded, his mind slipping back in time, to when he and Saoirse were still at his parents. Richard had been as good as his word, back in an hour, ready to head back for Elmton.

Ronan and Lydia had reluctantly hugged their son and then Saoirse, not willing to let them go but knowing that they had to. The younger couple was needed back in her hometown. That was a must, they knew.

Richard had sorted them out into the vehicle, Paul driving, himself riding shotgun as they say, and Silver in the back seat beside Saoirse. There had been little conversation on the drive. No one seemed willing to break the silence once they got started. Saoirse had been quiet, not talking much, her gaze focused on the window and the passing scenery. Rowan shifted his gaze between her and Richard, finding Richard turning frequently to watch her.

He had finally relaxed as they neared Elmton, thinking that they were safe. That they would be at Kelly's soon and then Richard would leave and head for home. He jumped as he heard the loud call from Paul and shifted to stare behind him.

Paul's call had startled Saoirse as well. She had jumped, her hand tightening on Rowan's as she looked around, brought back to the present in a rude manner.

Paul had struggled to keep the SUV on the roadway but was boxed in by trucks. The truck travelling beside him crowded him to the shoulder. He finally ran out of shoulder and hit the shallow ditch. The sudden shift of ground under the tires had taken control of the vehicle out of his hands. He fought the wheel, keeping the vehicle on its wheels, but doing little else.

Richard tried his best to store away any identifying information on the vehicles but it was all happening too quickly. Dust clouds swirled as well, hiding the vehicles from his sight. Silver's hand was on Saoirse, ready to pull her from the vehicle and run.

They never got a chance to escape the vehicle. Despite Paul's best efforts, the SUV slammed sideways into a tree, just in front of Richard's seat. He slammed into the door, a pain-filled cry wrenched from him. Silver hit her door and was silent. Paul was slammed into the steering wheel and lay draped across it, blood trickling down his face from cuts.

Saoirse had been thrown around despite her seatbelt and rested against Silver, her eyes closed. Rowan seemed to come off the best of them all, still conscious but very groggy. He wasn't able to make any sense of what had happened. He fumbled for his seatbelt, his fingers not working as they should and missing the latch for the seatbelt despite his best efforts.

The door beside him was wrenched open and he felt hands on him, pulling him out and then dragging him away. He tried to turn and go back, to find Saoirse but the hands kept him moving forward. He knew that the seatbelt had been sliced apart to release him. Rowan had heard that sound of tearing material.

Shoved into a motorhome, he slumped sideways against the couch in it, his eyes shutting against the pain that he was feeling. He didn't know who had taken him there but he just wanted to sleep.

Saoirse didn't feel the knife that sliced through her own seatbelt or feel herself pulled from the vehicle. She was carried to the waiting vehicle, her head lolling backwards, her free arm and braid swinging with each rapid step forward. She didn't know that Rowan was in the vehicle already or that she was shoved quickly inside as well, to fall to the floor and lay still. She didn't see the heavyset man who entered and stood over the couple.

The driver took off, leaving the trucks to follow him at a rapid pace. He took the road that encircled the town, not driving through it. Pulling into a farm on the opposite of town, he backed the motorhome into the barn and shut off the motor.

"This should do it." Gil, his name was, turned to the heavyset man.

"It should. No one can see it from the road, not in the barn. Besides, the house is set well back. I know there is not a lot of traffic out here, other than coming here. That is a plus." The man turned and stared back at Saoirse. "She needs to tell us where that information is. She has to have it."

127

“We’ll find out. Where do you want them?”

“The bedroom that we set up. I didn’t expect to have the two of them.” The man thought for a moment. “Yes, it will work. I need people to work the fields, doing the planting. They will do as well as hiring anyone. Evan is around?”

“He should be. You told him to be here. And he always does what you say.” Gil was puzzled. He wasn’t sure about Evan, not at all.

“Good. He’ll be their guard during the day. He leaves at night. That won’t change.” The man, Blackmore Street, heaved himself to his feet and moved to exit the motorhome. “Buddy will be out here as well. We need to keep an eye on him.” He left, not even taking a second glance at Saoirse or Rowan.

Gil shook his head. He had his own opinion on Buddy. He didn’t know him that well or even what his connection to Street was but there was something wrong about him. He liked his alcohol and his drugs too much, Gil thought, to be a reliable guard. That would fall to him and Dirk, he thought.

Dirk appeared at that moment, his eyes on Gil.

“Where to with them?” He hooked a finger over his shoulder.

“The bedroom we fixed up.” He stood for a moment, his eyes on Saoirse. He had a bad feeling about what would happen to her. He wanted no part of it, but the money offered him was just too good.

Chapter 36

Rowan finally roused late that night, rolling to his back, an arm flung across his eyes. He hurt, he decided, in every bone of his body and in every fibre. What had he gone and done that he didn't remember going and doing? He moved his arm and stared around, wondering that he was sprawled on the floor and not in his bed.

He sat up, his eyes closing against the dizziness that coursed through him. His eyes popped open at last and he glanced around the room. Frowning, Rowan lurched to his feet, a hand held out to brace himself against the wall, fighting the nausea that the very motion of rising had wrought in his stomach.

This isn't my room, he thought. *Where am I?* Rowan searched for a door in the dim light, the room lit only by the moonlight coming through the dirty streaked windows. He found the doorknob and twisted it. The door refused to open. He tugged at the knob and twisted and turned it, finding the door just would not open.

Rowan turned, puzzled as to why that would be as he made his way around the perimeter of the room. He stopped at each of the two windows, unable to raise them. He scraped at the dirt and stared outside, not recognizing where he was.

Lord? Where am I? And why do I feel like I do? He slumped back against the door, his head resting against it. His eyes closed as he fought a headache and the nausea. He lifted his head again as he heard a soft sound and his eyes searched the dimness that they were growing accustomed to.

On his hands and knees, he crawled towards a mattress on the floor, his hands reaching for the body. Rowan drew in a deep breath as he recognized Saoirse.

"Saoirse? Wake up, sweetheart." Rowan tried his best to rouse her to no avail. He sat cross-legged on the floor, gathering her to him, reaching for a blanket to wrap around her. "Come on, sweetheart. Wake up for me."

He finally dozed off, his head resting against her, his headache still pounding. He had no idea what the time of night it was. His watch had been broken in the impact with a door during the accident.

Rousing in the early morning light, Rowan shielded his eyes from the bright light that shone at him. He shook his head at the words that he could not understand. Pulled roughly to his feet, he set Saoirse on hers, keeping an arm around her as she swayed.

Saoirse had roused as she heard the rough voice ordering them to their feet. She was disoriented, not knowing where she was or who it was that held her. She finally recognized Rowan's voice as he answered the questions pelted at him. She shivered in the coolness of the morning before Rowan's arm tightened around her.

"Out here." The voice behind the light was getting angry. "I only say it once and you obey. Do you get me?"

"We do." Rowan walked towards the light, following it as Gil backed away and towards the kitchen. "What do you want with us?"

Gil turned off the flashlight and set it down before he glared at them. His finger pointed towards Saoirse.

"She cooks for us. You? You sit."

"She's been hurt. She can't cook for you."

"Yes, she can." Gil reached out a hand and roughly tore Saoirse from Rowan's grip, despite her cry of pain. "Cook, woman, if you know what's good for you."

Saoirse stared at him, blinking against the pain that she felt before she moved to do just that. She stared into the fridge before reaching for the ham and eggs and starting the meal, her movements slow and stilted.

"Hurry up. We don't have all day. You two need to be out in the fields shortly."

———

130

"Fields? What are you talking about?" Rowan stood, trying to get around Gil to Saoirse before he paused, his hands rising. "You don't need a gun, man."

"I do. You, sit like you were told to. I won't hesitate to shoot either one of you if you don't."

Rowan caught Saoirse's eye and the slight shake of her head and sighed. *This is working out well, Lord. Now what?* He sank into the chair he had vacated so quickly, his eyes on Gil and the gun he was holding on Saoirse. He saw that Saoirse was in pain and trying to move as quickly as she could. *Lord, please? Help us to escape. Heal my sweetheart.*

The meal finished, Rowan helped to clear the kitchen before he felt the prod of the gun into his back. He looked over his shoulder, a shudder running through him at the evil he sensed coming from Gil.

"Outside. Both of you. Time's wasting. You need to be in the fields. The seedlings are ready to be planted."

Saoirse's hand was on her head as she fought her headache.

"I don't understand. What fields? What seedlings?"

"You'll see. As of now, you are our unpaid labour, until Mr. Street says otherwise. A full day is what will be expected from you. You will be under guard. Do you understand that?"

Rowan and Saoirse exchanged glances before they nodded. Rowan sighed to himself. So much for escaping, even if they had been able to run, and he highly doubted that either of them was able to at the moment.

The sun was hot and scorching in the spring day, beating down on the two. Their bodies aching from the accident, they could only move so quickly. Gil would appear and disappear, his words lashing at them for not being further along than they were. The guard that was there with them, Evan, Rowan thought his name was, was more compassionate, providing water for them and then sandwiches for their lunch. Saoirse was too exhausted to eat, drinking only the water provided, her body leaning against Rowan as it sagged from the pain and the unaccustomed work.

Night was falling as Gil reappeared, his gun out to direct them back to the house. Saoirse's feet dragged as she climbed the steps.

"Now, woman. Prepare our meal." Gil's smirk said it all. She would receive no relief from that.

"Leave her be. She can hardly move." Rowan's protest brought the gun towards himself.

"She'll cook or you die. She can take her pick. You? Back into that chair."

Saoirse and Rowan exchanged a glance before she wearily picked up the potato peeler to peel the potatoes and then slice them into a pot of salted water, to go onto the stove to cook. The steaks were set under the broiler and a tossed salad was prepared. She was too weary to eat much and saw that Rowan didn't eat a lot either. He was allowed to help her clean up the mess in the kitchen before they were once more locked into the bedroom. She sank onto the mattress, not feeling the blanket that Rowan tucked over her before he wrapped himself in one and laid down in front of the door. No one was getting in, he thought, not past him even if he was asleep.

Chapter 37

The next two days followed the same pattern. Roused early in the morning, before it became light, Saoirse was forced to prepare breakfast for them all. The meal now included not just herself and Rowan but also Gil, Dirk, and Buddy. She moved carefully as she worked away, her headache starting to diminish but her body aching. Rowan was forced to sit and watch, the gun in Gil's hand pointed at his head.

Rowan watched Saoirse carefully, compassion in his gaze when she caught his eye and something else that she frowned at. He had shaken his head slightly at her, his eyes flickering towards Gil and then back again. He wasn't sure about the other two, just what their role was, but he refused to do anything that would harm her. Rowan knew in his heart that she was the one for him, his sweetheart for life as he now thought of her. His love for her was growing each day. Only he couldn't tell her that. He could only send glances to her and hope that she could read in them his love for her.

Saoirse sat beside Rowan that third day, leaning against him as she twisted the water bottle in her hands. The sun had been brutal beating down on them that day. She felt the sunburn on her face and arms and knew that the skin would peel soon. It always did with her. Her skin was fair enough that she rarely tanned, only burnt, peeled, and burnt again.

"What do you think is going on?" Her voice was low as she asked Rowan that question. Her eyes were on Evan as he sat about fifteen feet from them, leaning back against a tree.

Rowan took a bite of his sandwich and chewed it. He swallowed before he spoke, his mind racing as to the possibilities.

"I don't know, sweetheart. I really don't. Maybe it has to do with those parcels Bill found. Maybe something else." He tilted his head to study her face. "God is still here, sweetheart."

"I know that, Rowan. It's just so hard to see that." She looked up at him, her words stopping for a moment as she caught a glimpse of their future, together. She knew then that she was in love with Rowan, would be for the rest of her life. Only Saoirse had no hope that it would ever come to anything. "Where is God, Rowan? I don't see Him here."

"He is here, sweetheart. He has promised to never leave us or forsake us. He fights our battles for us. He is still here. That I know. Even with what I went through before, He was there. I know that I shut down. You saw that. I shut down to protect myself but God spoke to me every day. His message was to wait. To wait for His timing. He brought you and Connell in at the right time. I don't know who or why I was locked up. God does. Even if I never know here on earth, God brought you into my life. I never want to lose you." Rowan's heart was in his voice and on his face and in his eyes as he looked down at her.

Saoirse leaned a little bit harder against him before she sighed, seeing Evan rising to his feet.

"We have to get back to work, Rowan. Thank you for reminding me. It's hard to think of that, you know." She took the hand that Rowan extended to her as he rose and they walked hand in hand back to the fields.

Rowan's head shot around that evening as he sat in the kitchen, hearing another voice. He frowned. The voice sounded familiar but he had no idea why. He watched as the heavyset older man entered the kitchen and frowned. *Now what, Lord,* he questioned. *Who is he and why is he here? I don't like that he's letting us see his face. That usually means we don't walk out of here.*

Street stared around, a sense of satisfaction in him. He had spoken with Evan who told him that the fields were being planted. The pair were slow, he said, but given the accident and their injuries, the heat from the spring sun, and their lack of knowledge, he felt it was going fine. Street had nodded, not bothering to walk through to the fields. That would be too much work for him. Evan had watched him, hiding the disgust that he felt towards his employer.

Watching Saoirse, Street had nodded. *Yes,* he thought, *she is where I want her. Beaten down. Not willing to fight. Now, this young man.* He turned to study Rowan, finding his steady eyes on him, assessing him and finding him wanting. Street felt the anger growing in him towards Rowan and decided that Rowan would not walk away. Not ever.

Rowan rose, despite the men in the kitchen, and positioned himself between Saoirse and the others. It was a deliberate act, he knew, and one that could bring consequences against himself or Saoirse, but he had to protect her. That much was certain. He had caught the looks Buddy was sending her way and feared for his sweetheart.

The meal over, Rowan and Saoirse cleared away the remnants and the dishes and turned to head from the room. Street stopped them with a raised hand.

"Where is it, Saoirse?" Street glared at her in anger. "Where is it?"

"Where is what?" Saoirse shook her head. "I don't know what you mean. I have nothing that you would want."

"Oh, but you do. You do, young lady. And you will tell me where it is."

Saoirse simply shook her head. "I don't know what you want. I have nothing. I brought nothing back from down south if that's what you mean. Sorry." She headed away from him, leaving him sputtering in anger.

Rowan followed, the package of baking soda in his hand that he had taken from the kitchen cabinet. He heard the door lock behind them before he headed for the small ensuite, making a paste of the baking soda and water.

"Saoirse? Here. Spread this over your face and arms. It will feel dry after a while, but it will help with the burning."

"Thank you, Rowan. I hadn't thought of that but I didn't think I could get away with taking it."

"Not a choice, Saoirse. I just took it." Rowan walked away, closing the door being him and giving her privacy. He stood at one of the windows, a hand resting against the glass, as he stared out, frowning as he saw Evan standing staring back. He saw Evan's hand raised slightly before the other man headed for his vehicle and drove away. He felt a sense of loss when Evan did and didn't or couldn't understand that.

Chapter 38

The pattern continued over the next week or so. Saoirse and Rowan were up before dawn and then out into the fields to continue planting and watering. It made no difference if it was sunny or drizzling rain. The one day that it rained hard, they were allowed to stay out of the fields but Saoirse was made to clean the house. She stared in disgust before she dug into her work. Rowan worked alongside her, ignoring Gil's orders to let the woman do it on her own. He had simply stood and stared Gil down. Gil had turned away, discomfort inside him at allowing Saoirse to clean but he had shrugged. That was a woman's work, he decided, not a man's.

About two weeks after their abduction, Saoirse turned from the counter where she had been tidying up after breakfast. It was raining and that meant they could not be in the fields. She sighed to herself. That meant a day locked into the room. Not that she minded too much. She could use the rest but she worried about Rowan. She felt herself starting to shut down and had no idea how it was affecting him. She could see it was to some extent but he had a peace about their situation that she had not yet achieved.

Buddy stood in front of her, swaying on his feet. She backed away from him, the stench of the alcohol that he had consumed strong on his breath. She saw Rowan standing behind him, fists clenched at his sides as he watched intently.

"You're mine, you know that." Buddy reached out a hand to grasp her wrist despite her struggles to escape him. "Street says that you're mine. Today, it's our wedding day. Did you know that?" His words were slurred together and she had to listen hard to understand.

"No, it's not. I'm not marrying you." Saoirse struggled harder and harder to escape the iron grasp on her wrist.

"Oh, you are." Buddy leered at her, thinking he was smiling. "You're mine, Street says."

———

Rowan's hand on Buddy's shoulder pulled him away from Saoirse. She stood, horrified as she watched Buddy, a hand rubbing at the wrist. She knew that it would be bruised.

"She's not yours, Buddy. She makes her own choice as to who she marries. No one does that for her." Rowan backed away, Buddy following him.

"No, she's mine." Buddy was belligerent, his voice rising in anger. "She's mine." He swung at Rowan, missing and his body spinning with the motion of that action, barely able to keep upright.

"Not happening. Not a chance." Rowan watched carefully as Buddy spied Saoirse again and turned that way. He sighed. *He's not giving me any choice, is he?* "Buddy?"

Buddy turned again, anger flaring. "Stay out of this." His words were becoming more slurred as he spoke. "She's mine. Street said so." He swung at Rowan again.

Rowan had finally had enough. His closed fist connected with Buddy's jaw and sent the other man to the floor, where he lay sprawled facedown. Rowan simply stepped over him and gathered Saoirse close to him, holding her as she shook in fear.

Evan stood watching, his eyes moving between Rowan and Buddy. He saw the outright fear, no terror, he thought, on Saoirse's face and sighed. He finally spoke.

"Rowan? Saoirse? This way, please." He didn't wait for them to respond, simply turned and walked into what would be the living room, although it was unrecognizable as such.

Rowan's arm around his sweetheart, he led Saoirse after him, not even taking a look at Buddy, who slept in his drunken slumber. He frowned as he saw the older couple who stood there, uncertainty in their demeanour.

"Rowan. Saoirse. This is a minister and his wife. I was to bring them here today. Saoirse, I'm sorry. I didn't know that was what Street had in mind. To marry you to Buddy. I wouldn't have gone if I had known."

"We understand." Rowan bit at his lip, his eyes on Saoirse whose face was upturned to him. "Actually, Evan, I have a marriage license here for Saoirse and myself. We had taken it out the day before we were brought here." Rowan was as careful in choosing his words as Evan had been. "We could use that. If we marry, perhaps Street will let it go."

Evan sighed, knowing that would not be the case. He knew that Street was away, not expected back for a week and that his expectations would be that Saoirse and Buddy would be married. He could not let that happen. Not to Saoirse. He had watched her over the past two weeks, regret in his heart that he was part of keeping them captive. He knew that she and Rowan were in love with one another. He could tell by how they treated one another and the glances that they sent each other's way when they didn't think the other was looking.

"Mr. Brown? Will that work?" Evan turned to the minister.

Brown shrugged. "I suppose. I don't really care who gets married as long as the deed is done and we're returned to our home." Brown and his wife lived in a town three hours away and had been roused from their sleep by Evan that morning.

Fifteen minutes later, Rowan folded the marriage certificate carefully and tucked it away into a pocket.

"You'll register it today?" Saoirse's eyes were on Brown.

"I already have." He pointed to the laptop that he had carried. "I did that just as we finished. Legally, it's registered. The rest is up to you. Now, can we leave?" He sensed the evil in the place and wanted out of there.

Rowan watched as Evan left before he turned to Saoirse, coming to stand in front of her. He saw the sorrow and discomfort that she was trying so hard to hide and simply swept her to his heart, his arms tight around her.

"It's okay, sweetheart. I love you."

Saoirse's head went back. "You do?"

"I do. I think that I fell in love with your picture when I searched to see who you were. I needed to know what you looked like. I printed it off and tucked it away in my wallet. It's still there." He simply hugged her tighter, feeling her arms around him.

"Thank you, Rowan." She sighed. "Now what?" Her own love for him was too fragile yet to speak it out loud but she prayed that he would understand from her hug.

"Now what? I have no idea. I'm trying to think of a way that we can get out of here."

"Buddy's out like a light. We could leave."

"We could, but I have no idea where to go to. And in the daylight, we risk the others coming and finding us leaving. We need to plan this."

"We can plan all we want but will it happen?" Saoirse bit at her lip. "I'm sorry, my love. I didn't mean that." Rowan's attention was caught by what she had called him and knew that she loved him.

"I know, sweetheart. We'll wait and watch and take the moment to escape when we can." He turned her back to the kitchen, staring down at Buddy. "Let me get him out of here. Then we can plan a proper meal that doesn't mean that you're rushing to get it ready and on the table when you are exhausted."

"How's your head?" Saoirse had been worried about the headaches that Rowan was still fighting.

"It's okay." He returned from dumping Buddy into the living room. "What do you think Street wants?"

"I have no idea. We don't have anything. Other than what Bill has taken." She paled. "I had a horrible thought. The coffin."

"What coffin?" Rowan turned from where he had set the coffee to drip. "I'm not following you."

"We brought that young woman home in a coffin. It was sealed by the authorities. I think it was likely opened here by the medical examiner. What if something was in it? And it's been buried!" Horror showed on her face at the thought.

———
140

Rowan had stared at Saoirse as she mentioned the coffin and then his eyes slid closed. *Is it possible, Lord, that whatever it is Street wants is in there? We have no access to it. How would we? And have Bill and Andrew even thought of that?* He had simply hugged Saoirse again and said that he would ask Bill that very question when he saw him next. Saoirse had raised a questioning look to him and he had nodded and stated that they would see Bill again and soon, he prayed.

A week had passed since that fateful day. Rowan and Saoirse had continued their work in the fields, finding it easier as the days went by. The seedlings were all planted and it was a matter of weeding around the plants.

They knew something had changed when they walked into the house that night. Evan followed them, a frown on his face as he saw Street. He decided then that he would not leave. He sometimes had stayed for a meal. Tonight would be one of those nights.

Street had watched the young couple, a smirk on his face. He had had no chance to speak with any of the men. He was certain that his orders had been carried out and Saoirse was Buddy's wife.

He waited until the meal was finished and Gil and Dirk had left to do their rounds. It was dark, the moon covered with clouds.

"So, Buddy. You're married now?" Street sat back in his chair, the chair creaking ominously under his weight.

"Fat chance of that. I never saw the minister." Buddy looked up, anger on his face. "He never showed up."

"He didn't?" Street stared at Rowan and then at Saoirse. He caught the movement of her left hand as she tried to hide it. "What's this? Open your hand." A heavy fist slammed onto the tabletop, jarring everything on it in his hanger. "Let me see your hand. What's this? A ring?" He glared between the two, fury in his very look. "So, the minister was here after all. Buddy? What? You were drunk?"

"He was. I refused to marry him. He passed out and slept on the floor." Saoirse was defiant. She had reached her limit and was ready to fight. She could feel Rowan tensing beside her, ready to defend her.

"You? Who did you marry? Him?" Street pointed at Rowan. "You can soon become a widow. You belong to Buddy, not him."

Rowan's anger flared and he grasped the edge of the table, his hands lifting it up and shoving it towards the other two men. Taken by surprise, Buddy flew to the floor, to lie in a huddled heap, his cries of pain drowned out by the anger flaming from Street. Street had been tilting back in his chair and Rowan's sudden shove with the table had sent him backwards. He lay still, stunned, not seeing Rowan grasp Saoirse's hand and flee from the house, towards the fields.

Rowan had plotted out a course for them to run if he had ever had a chance to take Saoirse and flee. He hesitated for a moment to get his bearings, a fisted hand raised as he shoved Saoirse behind him.

"It's me. It's Evan." Evan appeared out of the darkness. He had driven down the road and then made his way carefully back, to stay hidden in the shadows for just such an eventuality as he found. "Go on. Straight ahead. There's a road there. I'll meet you around there." He looked around as he heard sounds. "Run. And don't stop."

Nodding, Rowan grasped Saoirse's hand tighter and began to run. They stumbled over the rows in the fields, Saoirse falling a number of times, once taking Rowan down with her. They had laid still for a moment, catching their breaths.

"Do you hear them?" Saoirse tried to see behind her in the dark, her words sounding low in the night even though she tried to whisper.

"No, I don't hear them." Rowan dropped his forehead down onto his outstretched arm. "Catch your breath, sweetheart. I'm trying to find that road that Evan said was there. I think though that we have veered off course."

"I think you're right." Saoirse sat up, ready to jump up and begin running again. "I don't understand him. Why is he helping us?"

"He never seems to have been a part of them, now has he?" Rowan was on his feet, brushing the dirt off them. "It's almost as if he was a plant here."

"You think he's an officer?"

Rowan shrugged, a sound alerting him to the danger that they were in. "Come on, sweetheart. Hopefully, we'll find the road and a way home."

They began to run again, this time through heavy grass that slowed them down. They couldn't find the road and Rowan was beginning to fear that they would be captive again. He knew that he would not survive. Street would see to that. And no one would ever likely find his body. That would leave Saoirse at Street's mercy and mercy was not what she would be shown.

A sudden cry was drawn from Rowan and then Saoirse as they felt the ground disappear from under their feet. Rowan's arms reached to wrap Saoirse to him as they tumbled for a few feet before he could manage to get to his back and then slide down the slope. He felt the agonizing pain as his feet slammed into something, the something that he could not determine what it actually was. He laid still, catching his breath before he raised his head and looked around.

Afraid to move too much, not knowing exactly what was around them, Rowan spied a small tree just above his head. He shifted his body in order to reach the tree. A hand grasped it and pulled them upwards until he could wrap an arm around it and hold them in place. His head went back as he tried to catch his breath before the world spun in front of his eyes and he lost consciousness. His last coherent thought was a prayer for protection and would God please send someone to find them and fast? He didn't know how long that he could keep his arm around the tree and keep them safe. *Please, dear Lord?* *He slipped away to darkness, his other arm tight around his beloved Saoirse.*

Chapter 40

Coming back to the present, Rowan raised his head, watching Bill as he studied his notes. He sighed. *It was over, that part,* he thought, *but they still were in danger. Street was out there yet as were Buddy, Gil, and Dirk. Evan?* He had no idea where that man would be but he wanted to find him and thank him for his help when they ran and for his kindness over the weeks that they had been held captive.

Bill looked up, assessing Rowan and nodding. *He's back,* he thought. *This captivity didn't send him back into that well of darkness. Lord, You were there in many ways this time. You protected them both.*

"That's it?"

"I think so. Saoirse will need to give her statement. But from my point of view, that's what happened." Rowan stared down at the hands that he was rubbing together. "I don't get it, Bill. Why us?"

"Because you have something, or rather Saoirse does, that this Street wants. And yes, we did think of the coffin. Connell and Kelly both mentioned it. We are in the process of obtaining a court order to raise it and search it. The father is fighting us on that but given this information? We'll get our court order, I suspect." Bill's head turned. "Saoirse, you're awake."

"I am." Saoirse sat up carefully and then rose and walked from the room. Rowan was on his feet watching her.

"She'll be back, Rowan. She won't go far from you." Bill's amusement came through in his voice and Rowan's head shot around towards him.

"Now, why did you have me do that?" Rowan's head had begun to pound at his sudden movement.

———

"Sorry. I didn't mean to do that. Now, let's finish off your statement. I'll see if Saoirse will give hers as well today and then other than for clarification, we'll be done with them."

Saoirse had returned at that point, a cup of tea in her hands.

"I want to do it. I was listening to Rowan's. Just copy what he said and I'll sign it."

Bill grinned at her. "Sorry, I can't do that. It doesn't work that way. Hang tough for about fifteen minutes and then we'll do yours."

Two hours later, Bill tucked away everything and rose, his eyes on the younger couple. Rowan had moved to sit beside Saoirse, an arm around her as she leaned against him. *Another couple in love, Lord. Please protect them. This is far from over.* He finally walked away, stopping for a quick word with Ruth and Lydia in the kitchen before the door closed behind him.

His phone out, he checked for his messages. Satisfaction flooded his eyes for a moment. The judge had agreed to the court order and they would exhume the coffin and the young woman's body the next day. He frowned and then sent a message to Lily, asking her to pull any records from the medical examiner. His frown deepened as she replied that she had asked for them and that there were none and there should be.

Rowan had watched Bill walk away before he leaned back on the sofa, Saoirse leaning hard against him. She had wiped at her eyes, tears of pain and fear on her cheeks. He dropped a kiss on her head.

"Rowan?"

"What, sweetheart?"

"What do we do now? We can't go out and about, can we?" Saoirse was terrified that Street would find them. She knew as well as Rowan did that Street would be out for revenge.

"We live our lives, sweetheart. We go out and about. We shop. We visit. We go to church. We go for walks. And I get to take my bride out for a meal." He hesitated.

"And we need to find you a house."

"Us a house, sweetheart. I'm going nowhere without you." He looked up as he heard footsteps coming their way. "Bill didn't say that we couldn't talk about what we went through."

"No, he didn't. But they don't need to know all the details, do they?" Saoirse watched as her mother entered, a tray in her hands, followed by Lydia. She could hear her father, Ronan, and Connell talking in the kitchen.

"No, they don't. Some of it I know we need to keep quiet. Just for their protection and for the investigation." Rowan looked up at Ruth. "You should have called for me to come and help, Ruth."

"No, you're not up to it. It's our pleasure, Rowan." Ruth turned as Kelly entered. "Kelly, we need to ask the blessing on our food. Then, we eat."

Chapter 41

A week had passed since Rowan and Saoirse had made their escape. Their lives were still turned upside down as they struggled to cope with their emotions and injuries that had been left untreated. Ruth watched her daughter closely, seeing the changes that her captivity had wrought in her and worried. She also worried about how the young couple had married, even though she could see that they were in love.

Rowan had searched for a house, not finding one that he liked. Saoirse had told him that he was too picky. He had grinned at her and then hugged her, finally kissing her as he had wanted to for so long. She had stood in his arms that day, her eyes on him, seeing his love for her and finally admitting that she loved him.

That night, she sat on the edge of the bed, Rowan close enough that their shoulders were touching. She was frowning, a thought burrowing up from where she had hidden it.

"Evan? What about Evan?"

"What about Evan?" Rowan had been thinking about the other man a lot too.

"Is he an officer? And undercover?"

Rowan shrugged. "I don't know." He sighed as his phone chimed and he pulled it out. "This is weird."

"What is?" Saoirse leaned over to study the text message. "Evan? How did he get your number?"

"Easy. It's on my website. He could have researched that." Rowan studied the message, which warned them that Street was watching them every day. That they needed to take precautions. And did they really have to be house hunting at this time? Rowan grinned for a moment. "He's still watching out for us."

"He is. He's so different from the others. You know, he was never there at night." Saoirse thought back. "I often wondered where he was."

"I think that you could be right. Bill can't say if he is an officer."

"And how did Bill know where to find us?" Saoirse was on her feet, pacing before she ran from the room, heading for the sunroom where she had left her own phone.

Kelly looked up in surprise. "Saoirse? What is going on, love?"

"How did Bill know where we were?" Saoirse's fingers danced across her phone, sending off a message to Bill. "Bill hasn't been around. How do we know where the investigation stands?"

"He'll be around." Kelly watched Rowan as he stood just inside the doorway. "Rowan? So good of you to join us."

Rowan grinned. "I had no choice. I had to follow her." His finger pointed towards Saoirse. "She ran from me."

"She did, did she? You can't let her do that, you know." Kelly sat back in his chair, his hand resting on his Bible. "Saoirse. Rowan. Can we talk?"

"Sure, Dad. What's up?" Saoirse curled up on the love seat, tight to Rowan.

"First, I just want to say how glad we are that you two are home. I know that we've said it many times, but we are so thankful that God brought you home. Secondly, your parents and Ruth and I would like to do something for you both. You married under circumstances that you shouldn't have. We understand the whys. Silas and Madigan have been around. Silas has suggested that perhaps you would like to redo what you did. Let him marry you again. This time, Saoirse, you in your mother's dress. Whatever it takes to make better memories for you." He held up his hand as Saoirse opened her mouth. "Just think about it, that's all we ask. Now, about your work? I think we'll keep you working from home, for now, Saoirse. Rowan? What about your work?"

"I can work from anywhere. I was looking over the loft in your garage." Rowan bit at his lip. "You have it set up as an apartment with a large room that would be ideal for what I do. I would ask that you allow Saoirse and I to use it for now, until we find a house that we would like to purchase and make our own."

"Ruth mentioned that tonight. It's yours. It's furnished with the basics, but we can add to what you need."

"I have my furniture in storage. We can pull from that. Dad said he had put in storage here."

"He did." Kelly suddenly grinned. "Did you know that your parents have sold their house?"

Rowan looked shocked. "They have? I didn't know that they were selling. Dad and I haven't really had a chance to speak in the last week."

"They put it up for sale when you were captives. It sold in two days, he says. They've found a home here to purchase and move in next week."

"Oh, wow! Dad's coming back to his roots? Mom has always wanted to move here." Rowan looked up at Kelly. "Thank you, Kelly."

"You're more than welcome. Now, let me share what I have been reading. I spent a lot of time in prayer and searching the scriptures over those three weeks." Kelly went on to share his heart, something Saoirse was used to but not Rowan.

"God kept you safe, you two, whether you realize it or not. You were never alone. He was still there, as He always is."

"Rowan talked about that one day, Dad. Said God would never leave us or forsake us."

"He's right, love. God is there every day. He also sent his angels to protect you. You had a band of them surrounding you, I have no doubt. It could have gone much worse." Kelly looked at Rowan. "Did they ever tell you what you hit when you slid down that slope?"

Rowan shook his head. "No, no one ever has. And I have wondered what it was."

"It was a rock pile, Rowan. A pile of rocks that no one can figure out why they were there. They weren't from the slope. Someone had taken the time to pile them there. For what purpose originally? Who knows. But God knew that they were there and directed your steps that way that night. You may not have made it to where you say Evan was intending to wait for you. But God directed your steps to that slope. It kept you hidden the way you had fallen from being seen. The rescuers had to lean over to find you. That rock pile kept you from going over the edge of the slope and falling into the river below. You would not have survived it."

Saoirse's face had paled. "The old Sutton place? They said that he had piled rocks up all over the place and refused to say why."

"I asked him one time." Kelly admitted to that conversation from years previous. "He just shrugged and said God told him to. That they were like the markers that the Israelites were told to erect on their travels. His farm was his travels, he said, and he wanted the rock to show his love for God."

"And they did. We saw some of them and wondered about them." Rowan hugged Saoirse tighter. "That's a good reminder to follow God's directives and leading, isn't it?"

"It is. If he had not done that, you two would not be sitting here at this time."

Chapter 42

Gil watched as Saoirse walked through the downtown area the next morning, his eyes shadowed as he studied her seemingly carefree walk. He shook his head. He had no idea how they had managed to elude Dirk and himself that night. He thought he had seen Evan in the shadows but doubted that. Evan had been long gone by the point that the two had fled. Buddy stood beside him, anger flaring in him.

"How can she do that? Walk around without a care in the world?" His words were slurred. He had taken to drinking more and more in the last week and that disgusted Gil.

"She's free, Buddy. That's why. You never stood a chance with her."

"I did. Street says she's mine. I'll have her as my wife. You just wait." He stepped forward to go after her but Gil's hand on his arm stopped him.

"No, not now. You'd only get arrested. In fact, you're close to being arrested for being drunk in public. Let's go." Gil's hand was firm on Buddy's arm and he drew him away, not seeing Sal watching from the shadows.

Sal slipped away, a quick look around before he pulled out the phone he had secreted on his person. A quick message to Bill and he had disappeared into the crowd.

Bill paused in his walk downtown, his eyes on the message before he looked up, beckoning to a patrol officer.

"I have word that two of the abductors are here. Let's see if we can find them." Bill saw Sal watching and nodded as he pointed out the men. "There. Those two. Someone has pointed them out to us."

"Them? They've been hanging around here for the last few days. The smaller one? He's drunk most of the time."

The two men moved forward, hands out to stop Gil and Buddy. Gil's face had paled as he realized that the law had caught up with him. He wouldn't be out, not for a long time. Street would not take any calls from them, he had made that abundantly clear. Gil doubted that Buddy would remember that and would call Street, earning his wrath.

Gil had refused to talk, other than for asking for a lawyer, as he was booked. He stood in his cell after the heavy door had clanged shut behind him and stared around, the first time his conscience had raised its head in years. He slumped to the bunk, his head in his hands, and thought through his life. He had not killed anyone but he had been involved in crime since his teens. That crime had finally caught up with him. He worried about his mother, knowing how she would feel. He had not spoken with her in five years but he kept watch over her.

Buddy, on the other hand, talked freely, his drunkenness allowing for this. Even when he was provided with a lawyer, who tried to make him stop, he kept talking. The investigator simply shook his head. Buddy had unknowingly solved a number of crimes for them.

Bill stood in Kelly's kitchen that late afternoon, there in an official capacity. He was looking for Saoirse and Rowan, he had simply stated.

"They're in the apartment over the garage, Bill. They've moved there until they can find a house they want to purchase. Can you stay for a meal?" Ruth turned to him.

"No, I'm sorry. I'm not able to. Cora's expecting me home shortly." He excused himself and headed for the garage, stepping into the apartment through the open door that Rowan was holding. "Rowan? Saoirse? I can't stay for long but I have news."

"You've found Street?" Saoirse had a hopeful note in her voice.

"No, we haven't found him. But we have two men named Gil and Buddy. They won't be bothering you again for a while, I hope." He saw the relief that flooded their faces. "Buddy is talking. Gil is not, not without his lawyer. And that has not been forthcoming for him. It seems that not too many lawyers want to be involved with his case.”

“Buddy would be drunk.” Saoirse shook her head. “Where did you find them?”

“Watching you this morning. Someone on the street saw them and called me.” Bill watched her face pale before it cleared.

“Watching me? So it worked.”

“What worked?” Bill was puzzled even as he watched Rowan nodding his head.

“Being out and about. To draw them out. I won’t hide, Bill. Not anymore.” Bill noted the change in her and frowned for a moment. The Saoirse that he and Cora knew well would not have done that. But then again, this was a new Saoirse. They could all see the changes in her.

“It was? Don’t do it again, please. It might not go so well the next time.” Bill’s voice was stern as he admonished the pair.

After he left, Saoirse turned in Rowan’s arms, hugging him tightly. She prayed daily for Street to be caught. That they could begin the life that they were talking about. That they could have the freedom to move around once more without endangering anyone. For safety for their family and friends.

“Saiorse? Did you really do that?” Rowan’s cheek laid against the top of her head.

“I did, but I didn’t know that I was.” She shoved at him as he laughed. “I know. That doesn’t make much sense. I didn’t know that they were there. I was watching for them. I had to go downtown for the office, to the post office and then to pick up supplies. Dad didn’t know until afterwards. He took a strip off me for that.”

“I’m sure that he did. He’s worried about you, Saoirse.”

“I know. And that worry is driving me to distraction.” She laid her cheek against his chest, listening to the steady beat of his heart, knowing that she was loved deeply and that she loved deeply in return. “Where do we go from here, Rowan.”

———

"We keep doing whatever it is that brings them out. Andrew called earlier, just to check up on us as friends. He did warn me that Street will be hunting for us."

"I know. That scares me. I have such a hard time trusting that God will keep us safe. I know in my heart that He will. It's the head that having the difficulty."

"I know what you mean." Rowan stepped back, his hands reaching for hers. "Please, sweetheart? If you're going out somewhere, make sure you have someone with you. A bodyguard would be nice."

"You've been talking to Richard, haven't you? And when does his team move in?" Saoirse's disgruntled voice made Rowan grin.

"I haven't talked to him in a few days. He's ready to move in if we ask, but only if we ask, or if Bill or Andrew ask."

"That's good to know. I'm glad that they're healing but it saddens me that they were hurt on our behalf."

Chapter 43

Rowan turned the next morning as he heard his name called and frowned. He didn't know the man walking towards him before his face cleared. It was Paul, only he hadn't recognized him.

"Undercover, Paul?" Rowan grinned at the hat and sweatshirt Paul was wearing.

Paul grinned. "Nope. This is the new me. Courtesy of Silver. She says I need a new wardrobe if I'm going to be out and about. She doesn't want me recognized."

"She doesn't, huh?" Rowan looked around. "Do you have time for a coffee?"

"I do." Paul headed for the nearby diner. "This looks like a good location."

Rowan laughed. "It is. It is police approved." He slid into a booth and looked up. "Good morning, Bonnie. What's the special for lunch?"

"For you, your usual. Hamburger with the works and home fries. For your friend?"

"That sounds good. Only hold the lettuce please." Paul handed back the menu and watched Bonnie head away, her saucy voice calling out greetings to the regulars. "A small town. I miss that."

"You were raised in one, weren't you?"

"I was. But my past life is not why we're sitting in this booth in this diner in this town."

"Wow, Paul. How about a few more "in this" phrases?" Rowan grinned, relaxing for a moment.

Paul grinned in response, looking up to thank Bonnie as she placed their food in front of them. "You like that?" He bowed his head to ask a blessing on their meal before he studied his friend. "How are you doing, Rowan?"

Rowan shrugged. "Struggling, as you can imagine. Hurting for Saoirse. She's struggling. She only lets me see that, keeping it covered for her parents and friends."

"If you need to talk to someone, let me know. I know of someone who has gone through a horrible ordeal but will talk with you. Now, I hear that two of your captors were arrested."

"That they were. They were actually watching Saoirse and someone noticed that. I would like to thank that person."

"We all have those we would like to thank but never likely will be able to. Richard is concerned."

"I know he is. He knows me too well." Rowan bit into his hamburger, his thoughts not on his food. "How is he?"

"Into physiotherapy. He'll get back all of his motion and strength they tell him. That's an answer to prayer. Now, he has some ideas that he wanted me to give you." Paul slid over a sealed envelope. "I know what they are. He wants you and Saoirse to study them and then call him. In a week. Pray over them is what he has ordered you to do. He will not talk to you if you call in less than a week unless it is a matter of life and death." Paul's face was grim as he spoke.

"And it may well be, is what you're not saying." Rowan sat back, staring down at his plate, his appetite gone. "And I know that. So does Saoirse. We pray for protection every single day for each of us and our family and friends. Street will not go away quietly. That much we know. But how do we stop him?" He raised suddenly worried eyes. "How many times has he done this in the past?"

"That's for Bill and his investigators to determine. I am sure that he has done it before. We do have confirmation that he was in that country when Saoirse was and when you were."

Rowan paled even more. "He was behind it?"

Paul didn't say anything but then he didn't have to. The expression on his face and in his eyes was answer enough.

"And I have to let Saoirse know, don't I?" Rowan was frustrated. "When does this stop?"

"When we catch him. Has Bill said whether they found anything in the coffin?"

Rowan shook his head. "No, he hasn't. I didn't expect him to. He's meeting with us this evening just to update us. Maybe he will then. If I can pass on anything for you to give to Richard, I will."

"Thank you, my friend. Now, let's pray together. We haven't done that in a while."

Chapter 44

Saoirse looked up from her work as she felt her mother's hand on her shoulder and smiled a thank you for the sandwich and cup of tea that was placed beside her. She marked where she was studying the financial report and sat back, her eyes on her mother.

"Mom?"

Ruth turned as she spoke, before she sat in a chair in front of the desk, her own lunch on the table beside her. "Eat up, Saoirse. We need to talk but we also need to eat. And we need to pray."

"I know, Mom. It seems that lately we have spent a lot of time in prayer." Her hand went up to stop her mother's words. "It's as it should be, but it seems strange to be doing it together. We usually do it by ourselves. I like that we are spending time in prayer."

"I know, love. It is strange but so necessary."

The ladies chatted idly as they ate before Ruth set aside her plate. She had taken the day off from her practice, specifically to spend with Saoirse in just this manner

"Mom? What is it that you wanted to speak with me about?" Saoirse rose and moved around to sit in the other chair beside her mother, feeling that she needed to be closer to her.

"You and Rowan. You're okay?"

"We are, Mom. He loves me deeply. He tells me that every day in so many ways. I never expected that you know. I never expected to marry. And I love him just as deeply. It is strange how we married but God was there that day. We already had the marriage license. The minister registered it right away. How did you find out?"

"Bill. Someone told him that the scuttlebutt on the street was that you two had married. Andrew looked into it and

———

159

confirmed it." Ruth frowned. "But how did the news get to the street?"

Saoirse opened her mouth to reply and then clamped it shut. *It was Evan, wasn't it, Lord? He was looking out for us even then.* She didn't see the quick look that Ruth shot her before Ruth too began to pray for whoever it was that had helped her daughter. She didn't need to know a name in order to do that.

"Mom? What else is it? I know there is more." Saoirse watched her mother with concern,

"There is. Dad and I have been talking. We want you to continue to work from here for now. I know you feel that you need to be in the office but even with security around, Dad doesn't think it's safe. There is too much traffic in and out of the office some days."

"I know that, Mom. I'm content to work remotely. If we were in the middle of some pandemic, I would likely be working this way. So, let's call it a preview for what we pray never happens."

Ruth laughed, shaking a finger at her daughter. "You and your dreams and ideas, love. But so true. It is a blessing that we can work like this. Me? I can't practice medicine quite that way."

"But you can do telephone calls and video calls, can't you? I know you and Dad have talked about the what-ifs."

"We have. But now, you and Rowan. Have you been looking for a house?"

"We have, Mom, but there hasn't been one that we really feel would be one that we want." She eyed her mother. "Mom? What did you do?"

Ruth smiled. "You have always liked the Allens' home. It's close to us, but not that close that we would be spying on your every more. Eva approached me yesterday and I had to pray before I spoke to you. They are wanting to downsize. Eva knows how much you have always loved their home. They want to offer it to you at a very reasonable price."

"They do? I never dreamed that." Saoirse stared at her mother. "It would be perfect. I could set up a remote office there. There's the large attic area that would work for Rowan." She reached to hug her mother. "Let me talk to Rowan and then we'll go see them." She was on her feet, running from the room, her work forgotten.

Ruth watched her go, tears in her eyes but happiness as well. She remembered so well when she and Kelly had searched for the perfect home and found the one that she was sitting in. *Lord, if it is Your will, let it work out. And it seems as if it is.*

Chapter 45

Rowan watched later that afternoon as Saoirse reached to hug Eva Allen. He had to admit. This was the perfect house. He had watched Saoirse as she had roamed it, the ease of old friendship letting her do just that. She had admitted to him that Eva and her husband, Frank, were old friends of her parents and like an aunt and uncle to both Connell and herself. He could see the love between the two ladies.

Frank stood beside him, a smile on his face.

"She's happy, Rowan."

"She is. She deserves to be after what we went through."

"And so do you. You've had two adventures that no one would wish on anyone and have come through stronger in your faith. I talked with Kelly a while ago. He said that you were withdrawn when you first arrived here but have opened up to him in ways that you said you haven't with your own father."

"I have. Things that I could or would not discuss with Dad? I can with Kelly. Nothing against my relationship with my father, but he understands where I am right now."

"He does. He has always had a heart for the younger men, to encourage them in their faith. I know your father as well. We were friends when young. I missed him when he moved. I am glad to see that he and your mother are settled here in town."

"I am too. I won't go back to my hometown other than to visit and that will likely be a rarity. This is my home."

"It is. It's where your heart is." Frank nodded towards Saoirse. "Now, the price?" He named what they wanted, leaving Rowan to stare at him.

"That's way too low, Frank."

———

"Not at all. We never had any family of our own. Saoirse has taken that part of our hearts. She and Connell. We'll do something for him as well. But this house? Saoirse has always loved it, wanted to have a dollhouse the very same when she was tiny. It's our gift to you, to help you get established as a married couple. We had that when we started out from our parents." Frank walked away at that point, leaving Rowan to stare after him.

Rowan turned as he felt a hand on his shoulder. Kelly stood beside him. He and Ruth had come along at Rowan's insistence, knowing that Saoirse would not ask but would want them there. Connell was around somewhere as well, Rowan knew.

"Well?" Kelly knew the answer before he asked his question.

"It's a deal, Kelly. It's what Saoirse needs, to help her heal. If she heals, I do. And they have a really good security system. Whoever set it up for them knows his stuff."

"He does. It's a friend from another security team, from Riverville way. That's his specialty."

"Who don't you know?" Rowan grinned in response to Kelly's grin. "I fear for her, Kelly. This is not over. We're looking over our shoulders all the time."

"I know you are. Bill says that the two men he arrested are still in jail. One with no lawyer. One with no bail money."

"That's correct. But Street is still out there. He and Dirk."

"Dirk? That's an unusual name." Kelly paled. "We just hired someone named Dirk."

Rowan blanched. "Describe him, please."

Kelly did, watching as Rowan's eyes slid shut. "It's him?"

"It is. He had a very distinct tattoo on his neck."

"That would be him." Kelly's phone was out and he stepped away to speak with Bill. "Bill will come around in the morning." Kelly had moved back beside Rowan. "He'll make the arrest then. He says he'll need you to confirm the identity."

"We will gladly do that." Rowan's arm swept Saoirse to him.

"Who what?" Saoirse stared between her father and her husband.

"Dirk had taken work with your Dad. Bill will arrest him in the morning."

"He had? Oh. That's why the name seemed familiar." Saoirse sighed. "When does it end?"

"When we find Street. And no, we are not going to drive around town twenty-four hours a day, seven days a week to do that." Rowan hugged her with his arm. "Kelly, you need to talk to your daughter. She wants to do just that."

"She does? Saoirse?" Kelly grinned as she nodded. "Still trying to be a detective?"

"Why not? Isn't that why I read all those suspense stories? To learn how to do it?"

Chapter 46

Bill stood and watched as Saoirse worked away at her desk a few weeks later. He had knocked at the door. When Rowan had answered and taken one look at him, he had simply pointed through the house towards the office, following as Bill walked that way.

Saoirse looked up, surprised to see Bill before she was on her feet approaching him. Her heart sank as she saw the look on his face.

"He's run?"

Bill shook his head. "No, I'm sorry. Saoirse. Rowan. He's dead. When he didn't show up that morning, I asked a patrol officer to do a welfare check. We've been doing that for the last couple of weeks. He was found in the yard of the house that he was renting."

"Dead?" Saoirse swayed even as she paled. "Then we don't get any answers from him. Where to now, Bill?"

"Can we sit and talk?" Bill looked around as he spoke. "This is nice, Saoirse."

"Thank you. The furniture is mostly Rowan's." Saoirse led the way back to the kitchen, a bright airy room. "We have coffee if you wish."

"Thank you. I do. It's been a long day already." Bill sat, glad to do just that for a moment.

Rowan had been watching him. "What else, Bill? It's not just that Dirk is dead."

"No. It's not. I can't tell you everything that we found, but he has been following you since you ran from them. We have photos, notes, whatever it would take to kidnap you again, Saoirse. Do you know how close he has been at times?"

Saoirse paled before she became angry. "No, I don't. How would I?"

"Careful, sweetheart. Don't shoot the messenger." Rowan's arm was around her.

"I'm sorry, Bill. I want my life back and it's not happening." Saoirse sat back against Rowan. "What else can you tell us?"

"That Street is still around. We have word that he has put out a hit on Rowan, but has had no takers. Not in town. That's not to say he hasn't gone to other areas and found someone. You need to be extra cautious, Rowan. And Saoirse. Word is that he still intends you and Buddy to be a couple. Only Buddy isn't getting out of jail. We have linked him to some murders. Do you know how fortunate you two were?"

"We know, Bill. We know." Rowan swallowed hard. "He held a gun on me and I saw the hatred and look of murder in his eyes. It would not have taken much for him to pull the trigger. What else, as Saoirse has asked?"

"Not much right now."

"What about that coffin?" Saoirse shared a look with Rowan. "You have not said anything about it."

"No, and I can't. Not at the moment. It's under investigation. There should have been a medical examination done at the time her body was returned here and that wasn't done. That is under investigation by the powers that look after that. We did find something but I can't divulge exactly what it is."

"I thought you would." Rowan shook his head. "And if that is what Street is after, he'll never get it."

"No, he won't. But he will try. That's why you two have to take the precautions that we have laid out for you. If it becomes necessary, we will put you somewhere he can't find you."

"And that would never solve it, now would it?" Saoirse was on her feet, almost running from the room.

Rowan stood and stared after her before he looked back at Bill. He resumed his seat.

"What didn't you say, Bill?"

Bill sighed. Rowan was starting to know him only too well.

"That Street knows you are living here. Someone has been watching you too closely. Dirk never had a chance. That much I can tell you. It was a hit. We are working to see if it was Street that organized that. I can't emphasize enough how much care you two need to take."

"We know, Bill. We know. Kelly said that Dirk never appeared again and that you had been looking for him."

"We had. I was back there this morning, hoping that he had appeared. That's when I sent the patrol officer his way once more." Bill stared down at his empty cup. "What else can we do for you two?"

"Not a lot, I don't think. You have been doing your best." Rowan hesitated. "Make sure you take the time you need for Cora and Michael."

"I am, Rowan. Andrew is making sure of that. Now that he is a father, he understands much more how important that time is."

"He would." Rowan watched his friend. "You're troubled, Bill."

"I am, Rowan. And Saoirse? Can you come back and sit with Rowan? We still need to talk."

Chapter 47

Rowan raised his hands slowly, his eyes on Street as he stood in front of him, a gun pointed at Rowan's heart. He had come to the downtown area that morning, looking for inspiration in the decrepit buildings. He had been asked for a specific type of photo. Rowan now wondered if it had been Street who had approached him.

"Thank you, Rowan." Street smirked at him. "On your own. That is just what we wanted." He looked past Rowan. "Ross is behind you. Now, you will back up slowly and then we'll be on our way."

Rowan searched the area, looking for anyone who could help and not seeing anyone. He sighed to himself. He just had to come on his own, didn't he? Even Saoirse had still been sleeping when he had slipped quietly from the house. It was still early morning. He had wanted to catch a certain light.

"The camera, Rowan. Hand it over." Street took it and dropped it, watching as it smashed on the pavement. "Such a shame to lose such an expensive toy. Now, move!" His voice seemed to thunder in the early morning air.

Sal watched from the shadows, as Rowan backed away from Street and had his hands bound behind him before he was shoved into a waiting vehicle. He watched as well as Street stood, searching the area, seeming to feel eyes on him before he too was seated in the vehicle and the vehicle driven away.

Reaching for the phone that he had secreted, Sal sent off a text message to both Bill and Andrew. They would know what to do. He ran for his own vehicle, a ramshackle old car that ran better than it looked. He followed Street's vehicle as closely as he dared. Sal frowned. He wasn't heading out of town as he suspected. Instead, he was driving towards the opposite side.

Sal parked his car down the street from the luxury home that Street's vehicle had approached. It was vacant, Sal knew. He knew the vacant houses in town. He crouched down as he ran towards the gate, sliding through as it was closing and then heading for the shrubbery that ran along the driveway.

Rowan's heart fell as he saw the gate closing behind them. *How would anyone find him now? A third captivity? Lord, I thought that you and I had an agreement. No more captivity. Not for him at least.*

Pulled roughly from the vehicle, Rowan was shoved around the house and towards an outbuilding. He tried to fight his way free but the bonds on his wrists and the tight grip on his arm prevented that. *Lord, I can't do anything. I know that You are here. Protect me, please Lord. Let me go back to my sweetheart. Protect her. Don't let harm come to her. And if it is Your will that I don't go back to her, comfort her.*

Rowan was forced into a dark room with no windows and the door was slammed shut behind him. He heard the snick of a padlock as it snapped shut. He sighed before he sank to the damp earth. *Lord, it's just you and me. Guess You'll be the one to free me.*

Sal turned as he heard quiet footsteps approaching him and frowned at the man who appeared.

"Evan? What are you doing here? I thought you were undercover."

"I am, same as you. I saw you take off and followed you. I wasn't sure what was up." Evan watched as Street walked back to the car and then Ross drove off. "What's going on?"

"Rowan. He's locked up in that building. I can't tell if there are any guards."

"No, just Street and his bodyguard. Ross, I think he's called." Evan looked around. "What happened?"

"Rowan was on his own. Bill had warned him but he still went to the downtown area, on his own. Taking photos. Street destroyed his camera." Sal moved towards the building and then froze. "He has security on it."

———

"Yes, this place is wired well. I know it from a previous stakeout. We can't get in the usual way." Evan pulled Sal back into the shadows. "I know that there is a room inside that can be locked. Let me see if I can remember just where it is. We'll need tools."

Sal nodded. "Those I can get. I'll be back as soon as I can. You work on finding him."

Rowan's head raised as he heard tapping on the outside of the building before it began to be a concentrated tapping just behind him. He frowned, standing to move towards the wall. He turned so that he could tap back.

"Rowan?"

He could barely hear the whispered words and didn't answer.

"It's me. Evan. We're trying to get you out of there. Anyone with you?"

Rowan breathed a sigh of relief. "No, I'm on my own. But I can't help. My hands are tied behind my back."

"That's okay. Sal has gone for some tools." Evan's voice faded for a moment. "Hold on. I'll be back."

Sal ran towards Evan from the back of the property.

"The back?" Evan reached for the axe that Sal handed him.

"The back. They don't have security past the front of this building. We can get in and out that way. Did you find him?"

"I did. He's still tied up." Evan pointed to the section of the wall. "I'll start with this. I see you have a crowbar."

"I do. Once you get a hole made, that's when I'll do my work. And I talked to Bill. He's heading for Saoirse."

"Good. She's on her own, isn't she?"

"I suspect so. Richard was around yesterday."

"I know. I spoke with him. I think he said he was setting up near them."

"He is. I saw Paul and Silver watching the house."

"All right. Let's see what we can do for Rowan."

Carefully and as quietly as they could, Evan and Sal worked away to make a hole in the wall and enlarge it. Evan peered through finally, seeing Rowan standing near the opening, his eyes on Evan and Sal

"Let's get you out of there, Rowan." Evan's hands reached to untie him, throwing the rope back into the room. "Just can't stay out of trouble."

Rowan gave a grim smile. "It appears not. Thanks once more, Evan. I'm sorry we didn't find you that night."

"It's a good thing that you didn't. Dirk showed up and I had to hightail it out of there. I was worried that they would capture you two again."

Chapter 48

Tapping lightly at the door, Bill waited for Saoirse to respond. Her look of surprise changed to worry.

"Bill? You're here early. I was just having breakfast. Come in. Rowan is off somewhere with one of his cameras. He said last night he needed to catch some photos in the early morning light."

"Thank you, Saoirse. You've settled in here all right?" Bill took the mug of coffee she handed him, shaking his head at her offer of food.

"We have. I always loved this house. When Eva and Frank offered it to us, I couldn't wait to set up our home. It's close to Mom and Dad and also Ronan and Lydia but far enough away from them that we have our privacy. Connell is in and out all the time." She played with the plate of food in front of her before she shoved it to one side. "You're not here to just find that out."

"No, I'm not." Bill studied her, seeing the subtle changes in his and Cora's friend. "Rowan was taken by Street this morning."

"He was? Oh, no!" Saoirse sat back. "In the downtown area?"

"That's correct. An undercover officer saw it and followed him. He's working on freeing him right now."

"Okay. So now what? And you're not getting away with saying that we just sit here."

"No, I won't. I know you better than that." Bill leaned towards her, his forearms resting on the table. "We need to make some plans. This is where it gets very dangerous for you both. And for your families. Street may well go after them if he can't get to you."

"I know that, Bill. That worries me." Saoirse could barely get out the words. "What do I do?"

"We are working on that. Richard is here. Paul and Silver are watching your home. The others are with your parents. Richard is with Ronan and Lycia. He'll call in friends to help if he feels he needs to."

"This is putting everyone at risk." Saoirse played with her cup. "What do I do?"

"You do what we ask. You stay put. If we move you, it will be quick. Keep a bag packed with necessities for both you and Rowan. You won't have time to do that. Keep it in the door near the entry." Bill finally stood, reaching for her plate, and disposing of the untasted food before he slipped it into the dishwasher. He paused before he turned, his heart praying hard for her. "I know it's difficult, Saoirse. I've been there. I saw what it did to Cora."

"I know." Saoirse whispered. "Cora has talked to me as has Phoebe. Madigan told me what happened when it was still fresh for them." She rose, pacing. "What can I do that helps, Bill?"

Bill looked around as he heard the door open and close.

"Rowan is here. Talk to him. Stay put. If you need anything, groceries, whatever, let me know. I'll have someone get them for you. Lily has volunteered."

"She is a wonderful person, Bill. Thank her for me." She looked up as Rowan appeared in the doorway before she was across the room and in his arms, sobs shaking her body.

"Bill?" Rowan's voice was rough with his emotions.

"Just clarifying what you two need to do. Stay put. No more wandering around downtown on your own."

"I won't. But there is something that you should know. Street smashed my camera but I was able to upload what I had taken to the cloud program before he did. I need to go back through them, but there was something there that bothered me."

"Do that. Send it on to me as soon as you can. Just so you know. Paul and Silver are outside. Richard has people with Saoirse's parents and yours. If necessary, he is ready to move them away from here."

———

173

"Kelly and Ruth won't go. They have responsibilities here that they won't leave."

"I understand that, but if it means their lives, they will." Bill stared at the two before they nodded. "See that you do what we ask. We can't protect you two if you don't." He walked away, the front door closing softly behind him before his head dropped. They're not going to do that, are they, Lord? They're going to go out there and be targets.

Saoirse hugged Rowan hard before he reached to kiss her. They stood for some time, arms around one another as Rowan prayed for them.

"Rowan, what do we do? I know God will be there, that He can and will protect us. But we can't continue to live like this."

"I know." Rowan drew her into the office and then sat in his chair, pulling her down onto his lap. "Let me sort through the photos and send the ones I need to on to Bill. Then, we'll talk and make plans."

"I know where Bill is coming from, but it is our life that has been upended."

Chapter 49

Raising his head near the early morning hours, Rowan listened carefully before his head was back down on the pillow. He tightened his arm around Saoirse, who slept, her head on his shoulder. He thought that he had heard a noise but he must have imagined it. Bill was getting to him, he decided. His scare the day before was doing that as well.

His head was back up and then he was out of the bed, standing at the door, his head tilting as he listened. He was beside Saoirse, shaking her awake, a finger on her lips to keep her quiet.

"Someone is downstairs. Quick! Get dressed. We need to find a way out of here."

Saoirse was out of bed and dressed almost before he finished. Rowan turned from pulling a sweatshirt over his head and stared around the room. He could hear the cautious footsteps on the main floor. He frowned. Just one person, he thought.

"Where do we go, Rowan?" Saoirse clutched his hand tight. "We can't get downstairs."

"No. Or wait? He's moved to the back of the house." He pulled her with him, heading for the stairs. He prayed that they would be in time to find the door and escape.

Saoirse pulled him away from the front door, her head tilting as she listened. She couldn't hear the footsteps now and wondered where the intruder had gotten to.

"This way." Her lips were close to Rowan's ear. "The windows in the living room open like a door. We should be able to get out that way."

Rowan squeezed her hand as he followed before they both slid to a halt. They had not made it. They saw the large shape of their intruder in front of them and began to back away. Rowan shoved Saoirse behind him, feeling her hand clutch at the back of his sweatshirt and her rapid breathing. *Lord? I could use some help about now. Where do we go?*

They continued to back up, Saoirse's head turning to watch their steps.

"So, Rowan. Saoirse. It's just us. Alone at last." Street moved heavily towards them, anger emanating from him that they could feel across the number of feet that separated them. "You will not escape this time."

Saoirse continued to pull Rowan with her, heading for the kitchen. She reached for the door lock, snapping it open, and then yanking the door open. Rowan followed her through the door, Street right behind them. Saoirse stopped, unsure of where to go once her feet hit the porch floor.

"You're not going anywhere, Saoirse. Except with me." Street's weapon was raised even as Saoirse shoved at Rowan and turned, desperate to find somewhere to run to and hide.

She didn't see Rowan launch himself at the older man, his surprise move giving him a moment's advantage. But the advantage didn't last. Street's hand found Rowan's throat and closed against it as he raised his arm and shook the younger man.

Rowan's hands clawed at Street's as he tried so desperately to free himself. He could feel the darkness covering his eyes and prayed that God would protect his sweetheart. Rowan didn't see himself raised even further and then thrown from the porch, to land on the paving stones. He didn't hear Saoirse's scream as he laid sprawled facedown, not moving in the early morning light. The movement and his landing startled the early morning birds and critters and set up a flurry of activity.

Saoirse stood in shock, her hands covering her mouth as she stared down at Rowan. She heard Street moving her way and turned, running for the house once more. She didn't have time to slam the door and lock it behind her as she ran for the front door, her socked feet slipping on the shiny dark oak hardwood floors.

Street followed her, his cackle of glee at her distress sounding loudly in the rooms. He raised his weapon.

———

176

"You're not going anywhere, Saoirse. This time, it's just you and me."

Saoirse spun to face him, desperation in her stance.

"I don't get it, Street. Why me?"

"Revenge, my dear. Revenge. It would have been revenge enough for you to be married to Buddy. He would never have let you out of the house. He had assured me of that. But you had to have him arrested. That meant I had to come up with a new plan." Street paused, a puzzled look flickering across his face. "I have no idea how Rowan managed to get out of that building."

"He had help, Street. He had help. We have people watching out for us. Even now, they are watching."

Street leered at her. "No, they're not."

"What did you do?"

"Let's just say that their order of fast food held a little something more than they expected. They'll awake to find you dead. Rowan's dead."

"Please? Let me go to him." Saoirse searched for a way around Street and saw none. "I still don't get why."

"Why? You have something that I want. Where is it?"

"I don't have anything of yours. I never did." Saoirse could feel the tears of fear trickling down her face and prayed for strength.

"You keep saying that but you are wrong. You have to have it. I was told that you were given it." Street paused, a frown on his face before it cleared. "You'll get it for me."

"No, I won't." Saoirse moved suddenly, hearing the sound of the weapon firing. She flew backwards to land on the floor, her head hitting hard. A hand reached for her chest and she felt the blood on her fingers. Lord, this is it, she thought. Please comfort Rowan.

Street advanced and stared down at her before he began to speak in rage.

"Now, what did you go and do that for? How can I find what you have?" He had searched the downstairs when he first entered the house. Turning, he stared at the stairs to the upper floor before he moved that way.

A sudden flash of light in his eyes had his arm raising to block it. He barely heard the voices telling him to drop his weapon before he felt and heard the click of handcuffs. He was led from the house, not hearing or even caring at the calls for assistance for both Saoirse and Rowan.

Chapter 50

His weapon drawn, Bill moved cautiously through the early morning light towards the house. The call had come in from patrol that neither Paul nor Silver were awake and that there was a commotion coming from the house. Andrew moved beside him, watching as the ETF team moved in.

"Where are they?" Bill's voice was low.

"I pray that they got out, but somehow I don't think that they did." Andrew moved around the house, pausing for a moment. "There's Rowan. He's not moving." He was on his knees beside him, reaching for a pulse. "He's alive. But where is Saoirse?"

It was at that moment that they heard the gunshot and were on their feet heading for the door, the ETF team in front of them. They could hear the calls for someone to drop his weapon and then saw Street shoved past them and down the steps.

"Street?" Bill glanced at him. "That figures. Is he on his own?"

"He is." The ETF commander stopped in front of him. "But we need the paramedics. Saoirse has been shot."

Bill and Andrew stared at him before they were past him, standing over the officer who was desperately trying to stem the flow of blood from her wound.

"James?"

"It's bad, Andrew." James glanced up briefly. "I don't know that she'll make it to the hospital."

"Pray that she does." Andrew stepped back as the paramedics rushed in before he moved to watch another team working on Rowan. He walked down the steps to stand, his eyes roving the yard before they focused on Rowan. "How is he?"

"Starting to come to. We'll move him soon. The thing of it is, Andrew? He had strangle marks on his neck."

"He does? Street must have done that." Andrew turned as he heard his name. "Paul? Silver?"

"We're okay. Someone doped our food." Paul stared down at Rowan in horror. "Street?"

"Yeah, Street. We have him under arrest at last. But Saoirse was shot." Andrew watched with compassion as Paul and Silver took in what he had said.

"We tried, Andrew. We tried." Silver's voice had a quiver that she didn't even try to control.

"We know you did. He's been one step ahead of us the whole time." Andrew walked away, knowing that Rowan was in good hands. "Bill?"

"They headed in with Saoirse. I sent an escort." Bill looked around at the people who had started to gather in the dawn. "We'll canvas the area, but I don't know that we'll find out much. I sent patrol officers to their parents and to Connell."

"Didn't we just do this with them?"

"It feels like it. Listen, you head on in. I'll stay here and work with the teams." Bill stared at the house. "I don't know that Saoirse will ever feel the same about this house."

"She may not or she may just decide that she's taking back her life. We've talked over the years. She understands the chain of life and how God works in it. She's strong that way."

"She is, but this will shake her world like nothing else. The same for Rowan." Bill walked away, leaving Andrew pondering his words before he moved away as well, stopping to speak with each officer. He sat in his vehicle for a few minutes, his heart praying for his friends before he reached for his phone. "Hi, sweetheart. Did I wake you?"

Phoebe's voice echoed over his phone. "No, you didn't. I was awake, praying for Saoirse and Rowan. What is wrong? I can hear it, my love."

———

"I need you to head to the hospital. Saoirse's hurt bad. Rowan not so bad. I'm heading that way after I stop at the office." Andrew heard the sound of the closing door and knew that Phoebe was heading for her car.

"I'll be there. Andrew? How bad?" She drew in a breath as he didn't respond. "I see. I'm praying for you all."

Their parents waited anxiously for word, desperate to know how their children were. Connell paced the room, his off-duty teammates pacing with him. Cap had appeared briefly and spoken with him. He had arranged for someone to cover Connell's shift, knowing that Connell would do his best but his mind would not be totally on his work.

Andrew watched from the doorway before he moved towards the rooms. He spoke with the physicians and then walked to stand by Rowan's bedside. *He is fortunate, Lord,* Andrew thought. *You protected him. He could have been hurt so much worse than he is. But his heart will be hurting. He doesn't know yet about Saoirse. And once he does, nothing will keep him here.*

Rowan had roused, a hand feeling at his head and then his throat as he stared around the room. His eyes centred on Andrew.

"Andrew?"

"Rowan? You're awake. First, we have Street. He's been arrested." Andrew rested his hands lightly on the bedrail.

"Saoirse? I was so afraid. Where is she?" When Andrew didn't answer, Rowan shoved himself upright, ignoring the pain that he was in. "Where is she?" At the look on Andrew's face, Rowan's eyes slid closed. "No! Please, dear Lord! Not that!"

"She's still alive, Rowan, but she was shot in the chest. She's in surgery at the moment. They took her right there." Andrew stepped back as Rowan slid from the bed, a hand out to steady the other man.

"Mom and Dad?"

"In the waiting room. The surgeon said that he'll come to find you as soon as he can. The nurses will move you all up to the surgical waiting room now that you're on your feet."

Chapter 51

Two hours later, Rowan rose, his body protesting at the movement, and walked towards the surgeon heading his way. The nurse had been out on two occasions, just to update them as to the progress. She was not able to give much information other than that the surgery was progressing.

"Rowan?" Dean Ellis, the surgeon, studied the younger man. He had thought that he would be bringing devastating news to him but he had felt the power of the prayers raised over the length of the surgery.

"Dr. Ellis?"

"It's Dean, please. We're members of the same church family. Saoirse is in recovery. It went much better than I expected when I first saw her. God protected your wife, Rowan. The bullet did some damage, nicked some blood vessels, but it missed the heart and lungs. It shouldn't have." Dean's eyes saw the family gathering behind Rowan. "She'll recover, Rowan. Once she's in a unit in ICU, we'll come to find you."

"Thank you, Dean." Rowan's eyes slid closed as tears trickled down his face. "I thought that I had lost her."

"I know. And you yourself were hurt. You've been looked at?"

"I have. A headache. Some bumps and bruises. He tried hard to kill us, but he didn't succeed."

"No, he didn't." Dean watched as Rowan walked away, leaving his family to stare after him before Dean shook his head and headed back to the recovery room.

Four hours later, Rowan stood beside Saoirse and watched the medical equipment that surrounded her. He heard the beeps and whizzes of them all. His eyes dropped to her beloved face and his hand reached to cup her cheek as best he could with the oxygen mask in place. *Thank you, Lord. You have protected us and saved us. I don't know why You allowed her to be shot but You did. We may never know the reason for this all, but You do. In our finite minds sometimes we just don't get it, do we? Thank you, dear Lord, for Saoirse. She has brought such love and joy and fun into my life. I would be lost without her.*

He finally turned as the nurse touched his shoulder and nodded. He needed to leave but they would allow her parents and Connell in to see her. That they had promised him. He walked through the doors that opened for him and into his mother's arms, feeling like a lost little boy.

Two days later, Saoirse watched from her hospital bed as Rowan paced. She sighed to herself. *He's worrying himself to distraction about me, isn't he? Lord, we need to talk but I don't know how to anymore. Street took that ability away from me.*

"Rowan?" Her hand reached for his and he came and perched on the edge of the bed. "I thought that you were dead."

"He tried hard, sweetness. He tried hard. When I woke up here and saw Andrew's face, I thought that you had left me." He raised her hand to kiss it. "I was so scared. And lost."

"I know. All I could think of was getting away and getting help." Saoirse frowned. "He was still asking for whatever it was that I had. He also muttered something about revenge."

"He did? That's weird. Do we know anything about him?" Rowan turned as the door opened and Bill appeared. "And here is Bill. Maybe he can clue us in."

"Clue you in on what? That you're both alive and that Saoirse gets to go home tomorrow, she's healing that fast."

"We know that, Bill." Saoirse made a face at him. "About Street."

"Oh. I see. You want all the dirt on Street." Bill shook a finger at her. "We're working through it all, but I must say that God protected you mightily from him. He's a nasty bit of work."

"We talked, Bill." Saoirse paused to catch her breath. "Was Street even his real name?"

Bill studied her. "I have no idea how you knew that, but it's not. It's one that he assumed many years ago. About the time that your father left town, Rowan."

"He did? That long ago? Did Dad know him?"

"Apparently so. Listen. I just wanted to stop in and see how you two were. I'm setting up a meeting with everyone once you're home for a few days. By the weekend, I promise, Saoirse. Rowan, take care of your lady. No more adventures." Bill walked away, a wave of his hand as he did so.

Saoirse stared after him. "Did he really just do that?"

"He did, and he's right. You are heading home tomorrow. And then we'll find out what it's all about. At least, I hope we will." Rowan studied Saoirse, realizing that she had drifted off to sleep as he had been speaking. He dropped a kiss on her cheek and then found the chair he had claimed as his.

Chapter 52

As promised, Bill and Andrew appeared at Saoirse's and Rowan's that weekend. Their families had gathered around them. Silas and Madigan had asked to be present and Cora and Phoebe had just happened to stop by. Saoirse had stared at them all from where Rowan had seated her in the sunroom she adored and simply shaken her head.

Silas had led them off in prayer, first a prayer of thanksgiving and then a prayer for understanding and wisdom. The men had quickly followed his lead, Andrew ending their prayer time. He watched as Bill fidgeted in his seat, knowing that this was not Bill but that the conversation he would have with them would rock them all.

"Bill?" Rowan's voice finally broke through the silence. "What can you tell us that can't be kept in evidence until the trials?"

"Rowan? I am glad you phrased it that way. We can give you the whys and hows but you are correct. There is evidence that needs to stay quiet until the trials." Bill looked at Saoirse. "Saoirse. We've known each other for years. What I am about to say? You will recognize the players as will as your parents and Connell. Ronan, you will as well.

"Let's start with Buddy. He is in fact Street's son. Street refused to acknowledge that he was, having divorced Buddy's mother when Buddy was only a few months old. She was an addict and alcoholic. He knew no other way of life and followed in her footsteps. He came on Street's radar when he became an adult and Street hired him to do his dirty deeds.

"Dirk was hired from another town. He has no connection to our town other than Street. Gil is the same. They have both worked for Street for years. Both are facing a number of charges other than yours.

"You will ask about Evan. I am not at liberty to say much, other than he is an undercover police officer who was working to bring Street down. Sal? He's now part of our detective squad and a welcome one at that. Evan and Sal had kept in contact over the years, Sal being the one who would approach Evan or vice versa. That is how we knew that you two had married, Rowan. Evan got word to Sal." Bill paused to study all the faces in the room.

"Now for Street. Street is not his real name, as I mentioned. His last name was Blackmore." Bill paused again as he watched Ronan's face.

Ronan's face darkened. "Blackmore? He had as black a heart and life as his name. We could never prove what he had done but he was always one of the ones suspected for everything that happened in town that the teens were blamed for."

"That's right. I asked him one time if it was him. He just sneered at me and walked away." Kellys' face paled. "I turned him in one time when I saw him beating up another youth. I didn't think that he knew."

"He knew, Kelly. The arresting officer told him. He began to plot revenge on you. Moving away and then coming back under an assumed name was all part of it." Bill pointed at Saoirse. "He knew that he couldn't do anything with Connell. So he chose Saoirse. He's the one who also had Rowan kidnapped and locked away. He thought that Ronan had turned him in as well, you two were that close of friends.

"What he was looking for? There was a priceless artifact that was stolen from one of the museums in that country. It was to be shipped back on the plane but they weren't sure how to get it there. When the young lady died, the artifact was placed in her coffin. Only they had no way of getting it from there. The young lady? She died from an asthma attack. Her identity? Street's daughter. She never knew who her father was. Her mother kept that hidden from her. So when she died, he decided to exact more revenge from you. If his daughter died, then yours would as well. Only it would be a prolonged one.

"He had the idea of Buddy and Saoirse marrying. He felt that this would be revenge on you as well, given your upright

Christian testimony. He was dragging the dregs of the earth and thought anyone who didn't need to be removed.

"The artifact? It was recovered from the coffin and returned to the museum. They were thankful to get it back but horrified at what had happened to you, Rowan and Saoirse. The government has sent their apologies and thanks. There is also something else coming for you. I have no idea what. The prison where you were kept, Rowan? It has been destroyed. It was not a government prison, as you suspected, but one set up by rival gangs.

"Now, let's see. What have I forgotten?"

"The farm? The old Sutton place?" Kelly reached for Ruth's hand. "What happens to it?"

"Street had bought it. It was confiscated by the authorities. It will go up for auction but I know that the church board is open to purchasing it and setting it up for people in need of shelter and work."

"That's what we're working on." Silas spoke. "It is an opportunity that we felt we could not turn down when it was offered to us. It will help to clear the bad memories for both Rowan and Saoirse, I pray."

"It will." Saoirse settled down further in Rowan's arms, fatigue hitting her in waves. "Anything else?"

"Not at present. You will both have to testify, but we'll work with you. Phil has already stated that he will represent you." Phil Graham was a friend from church and a good lawyer. "He'll meet with you over the next few weeks."

"One thing that you never ever asked us about." Rowan spoke, his eyes on Saoirse. "Did you find shackles in the kitchen?"

Bill and Andrew shared a look. "We did, Rowan. None of those we arrested said what they were for. Evan hasn't either."

Rowan sighed, his arm tightening around his beloved bride. "We had to wear them, Bill. They would put them on us before we left the house in the morning and not take them off until we returned at night. We worked those fields, our steps encumbered by the shackles, for days. We had length enough for a normal step, but Gil delighted in taunting us that we couldn't run in them. That was the purpose."

The faces in the room grew grim as they all realized what that had meant. Silas' voice was raised in prayer.

The group finally left, leaving Rowan and Saoirse on their own. Saoirse slept, content just to be held in the arms of her beloved, knowing that she was loved.

Epilogue

Rowan was on a hunt. It was six months after the shooting and he needed to find Saoirse. Only she didn't see to be around in the house anywhere. He paused, a hand on the top of his head before his eyes lit up and his fingers snapped. The garden. Of course. They had just erected a gazebo in the centre of the rose garden and it was a favourite spot of hers. Rowan fingered the small jewelry box in his pocket and nodded.

Saoirse looked up as she heard footsteps, as always a slight chill running through her. She smiled, the smile lighting up her face. The little calico kitten that Rowan had brought home to her a month before curled up in her lap, her paws wrapped around Saoirse's hand.

Rowan bent to kiss his wife, moved away and then moved back in to kiss her again before he sat on the bench beside her, an arm wrapping around her.

"Have a good day, sweetness?"

"I did. Dad took it fine when I said I wanted to quit working for him." She leaned her head against Rowan. "I'm not sure what I want to do."

"It's okay. Take your time. You need this time. God will lead you where He wants you. I know that you have been back and forth to the farm."

"I have. I see such a need there. Perhaps fundraising for them is where I'll end up." She looked up at him. "What were you up to today, my love?"

"I found some beautiful scenery for the order that came through. My business is taking off and I'll soon need to hire."

"I'll do the office work for you. That will free you up to do what you do best." Saoirse grew quiet, her eyes on the flowers that were still in bloom and her ears hearing the sounds of life around her. "I never thought when we went in and found you that we would marry and go through what we did. Silas had a long talk with me the other day when he and Madigan stopped in. All about the chain of life."

"He likes that phrase." Rowan grinned. "But it's true. Life is a chain, our lives and situations and whatever linked together in our own lives and then linking to others. Christ is our anchor, the One that keeps us in place or raises to move us where God wants us. Is that how life goes?"

"It is. I don't know how people do it without God in their lives. Anchorless is how I would describe them. Street or rather Blackmore was certainly that." Saoirse grew quiet for a moment. "Phoebe and Cora were around as well. They talked about how they had to let God have their sorrow, their anger, their fear, their doubts. I agree with them. We have to let Him have those emotions and work them through for us. I didn't think of that."

"I had. I was going to speak with you tonight during our devotional time. Some wise ladies were ahead of me."

"I know they were. God was there for us, wasn't He?"

"He was. Bill called me earlier. The trials are set for next year. Dirk and Gil and Buddy have all taken plea deals. Blackmore hasn't and is refusing to cooperate with his lawyer."

"That's about the size of what I would expect from him." Saoirse stared around. "I love this place. I wasn't sure if we could stay here."

"We did. God helped us work through what happened to us here. We're stronger because of it." Rowan reached for her hand. "You only have that thin band I placed on your finger all those months ago. I love you deeply, Saoirse, more and more each day." He bit at his lip and then opened the little box. It showed a diamond engagement ring and matching bands for each of them. "Let me place this on your finger. You said that you didn't want another ceremony and I agreed. Just let me say that you are the half of my heart that I needed. God led us together and He will continue to lead us through life, no matter what we face." Rowan stared down at Saoirse, seeing the tears sparkling in her eyes, hearing her whispered words of love for him.

———

He kissed her and then just sat, their arms around each other as they communed with their Lord and listened to nature around them. He had no idea what would happen in the future but his hand was firmly in God's and he had God's chosen helpmeet in his arms.

Thank you for picking up the story of Saoirse and Rowan. It has been an adventure to write. I call my characters that people my books unruly and these two were. They threw in plot twists that I never saw coming.

The Chain of Life came from another book that I was writing. In that book, the comment is made about life and death and how it is the chain of life. That comment took off and thus this book.

I had no intention of bringing Bill and Cora, Andrew and Phoebe, or Silas and Madigan. They just had to walk in. Their stories are: *Hidden in the Hollow*, *The Potter's Hands*, and *Strong Courage*. Richard and his team appeared in other books and were welcome to this book, helping to move the plot along.

God is in control. God is still here. As I write in February 2021, we have just passed the first anniversary of the COVID-19 virus being in the world. I work in a medical office and it has impacted that immensely. God is there in this. He is working in people's hearts and lives. I grieve for those who are lost but thank Him for those who survive.

As we walk through life and face our own chain of life, keep your hand in God's. He has promised never to leave us or forsake us. Hold tight to His promises.

God bless.

Ronna